JANELLE SCHIECKE

Ghost Room

Emerald Link Press

First published by Emerald Link Press 2023

First edition

ISBN: 979-8-9886933-1-4

This book was professionally typeset on Reedsy.
Find out more at reedsy.com

I dedicate this book to my loving husband and my incredible son who never ceases to amaze and inspire me. You both understand my love of everything spooky and mysterious. Thank you for your love and support!

And to my mom and dad—I did it! Though you are not with us anymore, you lovingly supported me in my creative journey. I celebrate this with you both!

Contents

1

Prologue

It was dark and musty . . . disgusting, really. He could barely make out his surroundings. Once his vision cleared, he realized there was a bookcase in front of him. And it wasn't just a bookcase—it was vast and endless, extending upward and sideways as far as he could see. Some books softly glowed in an array of colors—red, green, purple, magenta. Many were barely held together—the bindings were torn and . . . wet? Yes, something covered the bindings; something slimy and shiny.

Just then, he heard a cackle. It ran up his spine and his hair stood on end. The cackle was uncomfortably close, and his heartbeat quickened. He could feel the sweat beading on his forehead and glanced down at the book in his hands. Had that brought him here? He couldn't resist the temptation of this house . . . this room. The stories alone were enough for him to bite.

As he was pondering his fate, one particular book caught his eye. It shone a vivid red and seemed to pulsate. He slowly walked toward it, the cackle only becoming closer and closer now. Quickly grabbing the book from the bookcase, he noticed it was warm to the touch and seemed to seep into him somehow. He never considered himself normal—hell, he was way above that. But this book? It magnified his condition even more.

He ran his fingers along the slimy edges and, as he did so, absorbed some kind of . . . energy. It was invigorating. What was happening to him? He felt invincible. Pure power ran through his veins. He knew he'd find something here but never imagined this . . . sublime rush of energy.

Suddenly, his surroundings began to fade and he was back in that room, alone. Silence engulfed him once more, save for his steady breathing. He felt more alive than ever before. And as he stared out the window, bathed in the soft moonlight pouring through, a large grin spread across his face.

2

Goodbye, Crescent Lane

The room I stood in was lifeless and stripped down. Bare walls stared back at me and the worn, cream carpet stretched out before me. The laughter, the tears . . . fifteen years of memories all stuffed away in the blink of an eye. I felt numb as I stood there staring into nothingness. This used to be my safe haven when I needed to get away, a place of refuge and comfort—a place where I could always be myself no matter what the outside world threw at me. Something that was mine and mine alone. And now what was it? Just a room, and nothing more.

Closing my eyes, I envisioned my room the way it used to be—a small desk facing the window with yesterday's clothes flung over the chair, friends smiling at me through framed pictures adorning the walls, and my old cross country trophies triumphantly displayed above my dresser. Sighing, I opened my eyes and wandered to the window, leaning my cheek against the cold glass. Our backyard looked like a magical fairyland with the morning dew glistening in the sunlight and a solitary rabbit contentedly nibbling at the grass. Faint visions of unicorns and fairies flashed before my eyes. I loved this view, and tried desperately to burn its image permanently into my memory. *Please, never leave me. Never leave . . .*

I hated the color pink. Why had I never painted over these pink walls? And now the sight of them brought tears to my eyes; I couldn't bear to leave them. A tight pang gripped my chest, and warm tears clouded my vision. *I'll miss you, ugly pink walls.* As I grabbed the handle of my suitcase, my mom called from downstairs.

"C'mon Jess, the moving van's all packed up—we need to get going. Now!"

I let out another deep sigh, and after one last look around my old room, trudged down the stairs, lazily bouncing my suitcase on every step.

"Wow, the excitement's killin' me! Turn it down a notch, will ya?" My mom was smirking at me from the bottom of the stairs, head cocked with hands on her hips. I rolled my eyes and walked toward the front door. "Dad and Ben are ready to go, car's all packed, and the moving van will follow us to Wicker Grove."

"Mom, I'm gonna *miss* this place. I can't leave. Everything's here! My life, my friends, my, my . . . my pink walls!" Yes, sarcastic—but true!

"Jess, we're not moving that far away." She held my face in her hands as I pouted. "I know, I know. It's hard for me too. This house has so many wonderful memories for all of us. It's hard to say goodbye. But we need the room and . . . It'll all be okay, I promise."

"I hope so, but . . . I just don't know. What if the neighbors suck? What if . . ."

"Is this helping you?"

"Is *what* helping me?"

"All the what-ifs? Is it?"

"I . . . I don't know. I *guess* . . . why?"

"Because, hun. That's all life is—what-ifs. If there were no what-ifs, then . . . what's the fun in that?

"Well, when you put it that way, I guess it makes sense."

"Then why don't we take this what-if and turn it into a yes? Yes, you will be happy. And yes, you will have great neighbors. And yes, you . . ."

"Okay, okay! I get it."

"Now that's my Jess." She smiled and ruffled my hair. "You're no pushover, hun. I love you. So let's do this, huh?"

I smiled as a salty tear traced its way down to the corner of my mouth. Then taking a deep breath in, I whispered, "Okay, let's do this. I'm ready."

"Good. We're all in this together. Never forget that."

Letting go of my suitcase, I hugged her tightly. Her warm embrace made everything seem okay. There we stood for what felt like forever in the empty hallway. And it was nice . . . the last quiet, special moment we would share with each other in this house.

Stepping outside, it was a beautiful spring morning and the luminous sunshine warmed my skin as I wheeled my suitcase to the car. Ironic—what a gorgeous day for such a life-shattering event. Didn't it always happen like this, though? Nature has a dark sense of humor. I had hoped for rain and storm clouds, but I guess you don't always get what you wish for.

I loved where we lived. Crescent Lane was quaint and lined with pretty houses, complete with immaculate lawns and gardens. When I was a little girl, one of my favorite things to do was race my friend Emily on our bikes to see who could get to the end of the cul-de-sac first. We'd pedal with our tiny legs spinning so hard, the warm summer breeze blowing through our hair and kissing our little girl cheeks. Smiling and laughing as we rode, the white streamers on our pink bikes whirled in the wind and the sunlight glistened off our hair.

Emily left the Midwest when we were ten. Her dad got a job in California, and the whole family had to relocate. We wrote to each other for about a year, and then the communication slowly waned and we hadn't been in touch since. Although the years had come between us, I thought about her all the time and hoped she was still as vibrant and happy as she'd always been.

"Jess, let's go!" my mom called from the front seat. "Hun, we *have* to get going—it's already ten o'clock." I snapped out of my daydream and realized I'd been staring down the cul-de-sac for some time, immersed in memories. After heaving my suitcase into the trunk of our SUV, I jumped in the back seat. Ben was sitting there hard at work playing video games on his handheld.

"Jess." He glanced up from his paused game. "You are *so* slow."

Crossing my arms and shaking my head, "You know what happens now, don't you? Little man, you're a sucker for punishment." I grabbed him in a mean headlock. "Say uncle!"

"Let me go!" he screamed, struggling to get loose.

"Not until I hear it!"

"Okay, uncle . . . *uncle!*"

"Now that wasn't so hard, was it?" I let him go.

"You're a turd."

"Takes one to know one." He let out a sigh of annoyance and got back to fighting aliens, or whatever the hell those things were roaring from his handheld.

Ben was my eleven-year-old little brother, and though we often got on each other's nerves as siblings do so well, I loved him dearly. As I settled into my seat, we began the journey to our new home. I shivered at the thought of having to live in a new house—a house where strangers used to live. Every house has a past and secrets to be discovered.

The drive took only twenty minutes, but by the time we arrived, it felt like we had entered the Twilight Zone. Crescent Lane had that comfortable family charm to it. As soon as you turned onto it, you could feel the atmosphere radiate like a warm and inviting blanket. Wicker Grove was entirely different. It didn't exist within a community of streets; rather, it seemed to fork off of a main road accidentally. Almost *too* accidentally—you could either continue on the main road, Belmont Avenue, or you could veer slightly to the right and end up on Wicker Grove. I didn't like it, and after glancing at Ben's timid expression, I could tell he didn't like it either.

"Mom, why did you and Dad buy *this* house? We looked at so many others that were so much nicer. This one is big and old . . . it kinda freaks me out."

"Oh, Jess, you watch too many scary movies." Mom was right on that one. "This house has the most potential. Yes, it's older, but that's part of the charm." She caught my uneasy expression in the side view mirror, and for a moment our eyes locked. "It's perfectly safe here, Jess. In fact, your dad was recommended this area by one of his good friends. It's really a delightful neighborhood."

Delightful, my ass. All the houses were century-old homes, and to top it off, they were all either white or gray—no yellow, blue, or green. Well, faded and creepy blue—I saw a couple of those. Wrapping my arms tightly around myself, I waited for the inevitable. Soon we'd be in our new home (our new creepy, rickety home) and there was nothing I could do about

7

it. I felt helpless and vulnerable—feelings I had all too easily anticipated.

As we drove down Wicker Grove, the yards became bigger and the houses were farther apart. *Oh, this is great. Who's gonna be able to hear me when I scream?* The houses on Crescent Lane were built just far apart enough so that, although you had a sense of privacy, your neighbors weren't too far away. But these houses—they weren't built very close to each other, and the yards resembled huge green pastures. I guess it was nice, in a way, to have a large yard; but the open space was a little much.

What I did notice, though, was that beyond the backyards of these houses there was a dark, sprawling forest. How far back it went, I had no idea, and I also had no intention of finding out—at least not any time soon. It looked like a jungle back there, thick with writhing branches struggling to breathe. All of a sudden, excitement and a hint of fear crept over me as curiosity slithered to the surface. What was in that forest? What secrets did it harbor? The unknown always intrigued me, and I knew I'd have to scratch this itch.

"Here we are, kids!" My mom's announcement jarred my train of thought and I blinked, a little flustered.

"Race you to the porch!" Ben jabbed my side and jumped out of the back seat.

"Ow, creep! That's it, you're getting it!"

I jumped out as fast I could and was just gaining on him when he jumped onto the first step of the porch, punching the air and proclaiming his victory. Panting, I bent over, hands on my knees, and regained my breath.

"I'll give you that one, Benny. But remember your victory will be short lived, my friend."

"Whatever, loser."

Swatting his finger away from my face, I said, "You have way too much energy, go put some of that into unpacking. And unpack my stuff while you're at it."

"Nice one—not a chance!"

Watching him run back to the car, I smirked. The kid sure had tenacity, I'd give him that.

My mom was shaking her head and calling for us both to get back and grab our things, which made me realize how long the driveway really was. It was a lot longer than the driveway we had on Crescent Lane, that's for sure.

"I'm just gonna look around for a little bit," I said.

"Okay, but your things aren't going to unpack themselves, you know. We'll unpack all of our stuff, so just bring in yours when you're finished."

"Okay, thanks."

"And be careful!"

"Mom! C'mon, I'm *fifteen*."

"I know, hun. You just don't know what's lying around here, that's all."

"You said it's safe here, didn't you?" I laughed.

"Jess, don't . . ." She waved a finger at me. "I'm tired and it's gonna be a long day."

Waving her off, "I know, I know . . ."

I put on my headphones to listen to the cassette of my new favorite band, Pearl Jam. Closing my eyes briefly and letting the music flow through me, I began my self-guided tour. The front porch extended the length of the entire house, and there were two white wicker rocking chairs, one on either side. There were five steps leading up to the porch, and the entire porch was painted such a bright shade of white that the sunlight flooding over it almost blinded me. The house itself was light gray, and the weathered vinyl siding was a bit old. I knew it was a fixer-upper when we'd looked at it before, but I hadn't noticed how much TLC it really needed until now. My parents liked fixing things up, though, and were excited to get a house with a little bit of character instead of a cookie-cutter like our old one. I guess I understood that. This house was definitely outdated, and next to our old house, it would have stuck out like a sore thumb. But its quirks gave it charm and personality. I'd just gotten here and was already warming up to the place.

Aside from the two windows on either side of the front door, there were two windows on the second floor as well that were situated right above. My parents said these were our rooms, and Ben and I could claim either one. Above the second-floor windows, there was a small circular window that was centered. The front of the house looked quaint enough. It kinda reminded me of the types of houses in the south, with their front porches and wicker chairs. The atmosphere felt lazy, and that was inviting too. No screaming kids whizzing by on scooters or cars speeding down the street.

The sun had begun to set and its rays gently crept over the rooftop, shimmering off the leaves of the large maple tree in the front yard. Yeah, I could like it here. I could get used to it.

3

The Doll

The house was a maze of excitement to explore again. My parents' room was upstairs toward the back, and it was colossal. There was also a large living room, a spacious and accommodating kitchen, a quaint dining room, and a cozy den that Dad said Ben and I could use as an entertainment room. My dad planned to store his wood crafts in the room off the foyer. He was a successful financial analyst, but spent his free time as a craftsman and made a small profit from the pieces he sold. On top of all this, a large shed stood in the backyard where my mom and dad planned to keep their tools and gardening supplies. My mom had a green thumb she was itching to use, and this yard was the perfect playground.

Ben and I made about five trips back and forth carrying our boxes from the moving van to our rooms. It had been pretty easy to determine which room would be mine. The rooms were almost identical, the only difference being the one to the left of the stairs had a walk-in closet. Although Ben had put up quite a fight about needing the larger closet, I had taken it over only minutes later and was hanging up my clothes.

"I'm a girl—sorry, that's just the way it goes. I have a lot more clothes than you do. I need the space."

"Girls . . . I don't get it. Why do you need so many clothes?"

I shrugged. "We just do."

"Yeah, well . . . enjoy. I'll enjoy my tiny box of a closet."

"Aww. Thanks, Benny!" I said in a voice people use when they speak to babies and reached out to hug him.

"Hey, I cut you a deal, so no hugs. Got it?"

"Ouch!" I clamped my hands to my chest.

Rolling his eyes, he turned back and headed to his room. I heard him laughing as he ran and did a cannonball on the bed. Our conversation was already forgotten.

We spent most of the evening setting up our rooms and organizing. For the first time since we'd arrived, it was starting to feel like home. It felt nice to have all my clothes and belongings put away in my new room, and I was slowly beginning to dig my new personal space. This room was also a lot larger than my room in our old house, which was a major plus. There was a large window in the middle of the wall facing the front yard and one on the left side. My bed was set up against the back wall, and sitting on it, I had a perfect view through the front window. My mom had bought a large fluffy pink rug for me that I placed on the floor in front of my bed. It was super soft and fuzzy when I walked on it with my bare feet. I had no idea why I'd chosen pink, but I guess it helped to have some of the color from my old room here. She'd bought Ben a similar rug for his room, but in royal blue.

I called down to my parents and asked them when we were having dinner since it was already six o'clock.

"In about a half hour, Jess. Dad and I just have to put a couple more things away. How does spaghetti sound?"

"Sure, works for me."

"Spaghetti!" Ben cried from his room.

We were Irish, but I swear Ben was a full-blown Italian at heart. He could eat pasta every night and never get sick of it. I always joked that he had a sweet tooth for pasta.

While my parents finished up, I figured I'd do some exploring. Between my room and Ben's room, there was a door that led up to the attic. Apparently, there was a room up there too. My parents said it was on a landing, above which you could access the stairs to the attic. Why was there a room there? Even if it was a storage room, that was a weird spot. Don't people store stuff in their basements or their garages? I opened the door to the attic and peered up the dark hallway. A chilly draft swept over me, and I immediately closed it. The hallway was almost pitch black—I could only make out the first ten steps or so until it got too dark to see.

"Jess, Mom and Dad said not to go up there. Plus, it's cold as hell anyway."

"Cold as hell . . . Isn't hell supposed to be, like, hot or something?"

"*Shut up*, Jess. You know what I mean."

"I know, whatever . . . C'mon, let's go downstairs."

After checking out the den, which Ben and I both agreed we would turn into the most awesome entertainment room, we walked through the living room and into the kitchen. The kitchen resembled the kind you see in magazines. It was bright and colorful with a blue country border lining the top of the walls. There was a long island in the middle, and they'd set up our table in front of a large window facing the backyard. The appliances were pretty old, but my parents would buy new ones soon enough.

At the far side of the kitchen, there was a sliding glass door that opened up to a deck spanning nearly the entire width of the house. Ben and I looked at each other, smiled, and raced to open the door. We had a small patio in the backyard of our house on Crescent Lane, but I'd always wanted a deck. To top it off, the backyard was about four times larger than our old backyard! While scanning the landscape, visions of summer badminton and volleyball danced in my head. How fun it would be to have our friends over, play some volleyball, and settle down for a nice barbecue on the deck. I breathed a sigh of relief as the tension this move had built up inside me began to unravel. I'd worked myself up into a nervous wreck, and for what?

"C'mon, guys! Spaghetti's ready!"

My mom and dad had set up dinner in the kitchen, and my dad was already helping himself to a huge scoop of tasty pasta. We were all settled around the kitchen table enjoying our first dinner in our new home when my mom asked Ben and me how our little exploration of the house went earlier.

"Can't wait to turn that den into a full-blown entertainment room! I like how it's kinda lower than the living room—makes it feel like our own little cubby hole or something. I mean, our own really *big* cubby hole." Ben laughed before wolfing down a slice of garlic bread.

"How'd you like it, Jess? And how's your new room?" my mom asked.

"I absolutely *love* my new room. It's so much bigger than my old room, and the closet is *amazing!*"

"Ha, we thought you'd like that closet." My dad smiled. "One of the first things your mom mentioned after we'd seen the place was how that room was going to be yours."

"Aww," I cooed, "Yep, mothers know best." My mom shot me

a loving wink.

"What's up with that room, though?"

"What room, hun?" my dad asked.

"That room up by the attic? And why don't you guys want us going up there?"

"Oh, we didn't mean to *never* go up there. Just wait for a few weeks until we're all settled in. It's so cold up there anyway, and it's just an empty room. I remember opening the door to the stairway when your mom and I first took a look at this place and the draft was just . . ." his voice died off as if he'd just remembered something.

"What is it?"

"Oh." He came back to reality after staring at the counter for what seemed like a minute. "I just thought it was weird because we came to see this place in September, and it was actually pretty warm that day. It shouldn't have been that cold up there." He shrugged, shooting us a curt smile, "These old houses have their quirks. Anyway—at least wait until I install a light switch up there."

There's no light switch??

"Speaking of chilly, who wants some ice cream?" my mom blurted out.

Way to change the subject, Mom.

"Me!" Ben cried out as she walked to the fridge.

As we ate dessert and expressed our excitement about all the new memories we'd make for ourselves here, thoughts of the mysterious room slowly died off.

It came rushing back to my mind after nightfall, however. As I lay in bed, I couldn't stop thinking about that room up by the attic. In fact, I tossed and turned amid fantastical dreams of opening the door and discovering a room full of gold and

15

precious gems. A pirate's treasure, secretly stored in our very own house. Stolen artifacts that had long been forgotten. Little did we know, we were on the brink of becoming richer than our wildest dreams! Then came the nightmares—visions of freakish monsters prowling the floors of our house with long, skeletal fingers. Their breath stank of rotten flesh as they opened their maws to reveal razor-sharp fangs dripping with fresh blood. *My* blood.

I awoke, my body drenched in sweat and struggling to catch my breath. *Gotta lay off those horror movies, Jess.* Closing my eyes, I took a deep breath in and felt my pulse return back to normal. Is this what I had to look forward to? I hadn't had a nightmare that felt that real in years. Maybe it was the stress of the move, or maybe it was the house itself. My thoughts returned to the room—that damn room. I had no idea what was up there, but its mere presence scared me. Even though it was hidden from the rest of the house (which made it even scarier), it stuck out like a sore thumb—like a nagging toothache that wouldn't go away. I had to investigate. When the time was right, I would. As sleep beckoned me once again, I closed my eyes; and this time I forced myself to think colorful and happy thoughts. Sleep came in no time.

The lovely sound of birds chirping was music to my ears when I woke up the next day to a bright and sunny Sunday morning. Ah, how I loved that sound. Eyes closed, I smiled and hugged the blankets tighter. Then another one of my senses awakened as the smell of fresh pancakes wafted into my room. I could hear the clatter of silverware and dishes as my parents set the table for Sunday breakfast. Throwing on my softest hoodie, I pulled my hair up into a messy bun and trotted downstairs.

My dad was already digging in and reading the newspaper. I grabbed some coffee and joined them at the table.

"So, how'd you sleep, sport?" My dad liked to call me sport. It was a cute term of endearment, but the older I got, the less I felt like a *sport*. I'd never object, though. My dad and I were very close and I knew we'd always be that way.

"Ohhh," I yawned. "I slept great. Tossed and turned a little bit, but just because of the new house and all."

My mom shot me a smile over her cup of coffee, "Oh, that'll pass. But it looks like the real snoozer right now is your brother." She glanced toward the stairs. "He's still snuggled up there in bed. Poor little guy. Yesterday was a big day for him with all the lifting and moving."

"Yeah, it's probably the video games too. He played for hours after dinner."

While he played video games, I stuck to my books and imagination. I guess you could say I had just as much inventory as he had, but in paperbacks.

My mom told us we could take a sick day on Monday if we wanted to. She said since we'd worked so hard during the weekend unpacking for the move, she'd play devil's advocate just this once and let us stay home. As tempting as her offer was (even more so because I knew this was a one-shot deal and wasn't likely to happen again), I really wanted to see my friends Amy and Max at school tomorrow and tell them about the big move. I wasn't sure if Ben had the same idea I did, though. He'd probably be more than happy to cash in on my mom's offer.

Amy and Max had acted kind of weird when I'd told them we were moving to Wicker Grove. It wasn't even the fact that we were moving to this new place that seemed to rattle them— when I told them our new address would be 274 Wicker Grove, their expressions change dramatically from excitement to those of concern.

That afternoon, my mom was working on gardening plans, my dad was setting up his craft room, and my brother was hard at work destroying monsters with his mighty controller. So I decided to explore the backyard. It was about four o'clock, and the sun shone brightly in the sky. Although there was a slight chill in the air, the sunlight was warm and it softly kissed my cheeks as I stepped out onto the deck. I surveyed each of our neighbors' yards, hoping to see something weird or even slightly amusing. To my dismay, no such luck—only the considerate wave of our neighbor to the left while he rode his lawnmower. I smiled and waved back, then walked into our yard. It was so vast, but also empty. There were no trees except a clump of four small pine trees at the far right side of our property, a few feet from the forest. I walked toward what my best guess was the middle of the yard, and just stared ahead at the tangled woody fortress. Trying to see through it was impossible. With all the snagging branches and clinging foliage, it was almost like a blockade.

The front edge looked to be a perfect line, as if all the vegetation mutually agreed to form a fortress of sorts. Then I noticed something toward the edge of the woods behind the small clump of pines—something light blue. With piqued interest, I briskly walked to where it lay. My heart was beating faster . . . *ah, the thrill of discovery*. Approaching it, I looked down. It was a porcelain doll. She had long black hair and was wearing a light blue dress. Her expression was cherubic and she had sweet rosy cheeks. Who would just leave a doll like this out by the woods? She was a nice doll—not one you'd want to lose.

"Jess! Dinner's ready!" My mom called from the deck. Dinner was early today. I looked down at the doll. It was eerily grinning back at me. I thought about picking it up and taking it inside with me . . . but, no, best to just leave it here. I'd be back.

"What were you doing back there?" My mom was staring at me inquisitively while she finished preparing the salad. I could tell she was curious. After all, she'd caught me digging my fingernails into my lips—a telltale sign I was in deep thought.

"Oh, I was just looking around and . . ." I shrugged, "I just saw something by the woods."

"What'd you see? It had to be quite a *something* because you snapped straight up when I called you—the kind of snap that gives ya whiplash." She chuckled.

"It was a doll—a really *nice* doll. It's porcelain, I think. Weird someone just left it there. Maybe it was from the family who lived here before?"

"Hmm. Well, I guess we may come across a few things here and there."

I was eager to know about the family who had lived here before us because they were a part of the history of this house. They had tread upon every inch of the floor we were now walking on, and had sat in this same kitchen and enjoyed dinners like the one we were about to enjoy. They had secrets, and their secrets were kept inside this house—just as ours would be. How long did they live here? Why'd they leave? And was that their lost doll?

"Maybe they had a little girl? Maybe that was her doll?"

She shrugged, "Maybe."

After dinner, we sat around laughing and sharing stories. We were all very proud of the hard work we'd done this weekend, and I guess we just wanted to give each other some mental pats on the backs. My dad, despite being a little sore from the move, had actually made some big advances in his craft room. Although the room was quite cluttered, he'd managed to get everything in there with some space to spare. We all listened as he talked about his upcoming project plans and customer requests.

Then it was Ben's turn. He talked about how far he'd gotten in his video game, and that he was able to save it at the perfect time because shortly after saving it, he'd been ambushed and had to start over again—but at his new save point. I listened, although I really couldn't care less. My mom talked about how she and her friend Gayle were going to go over gardening plans for the spring. She already had an idea of what she was going to plant and where, and she was also excited about growing her first-ever vegetable garden.

I just smiled and took it all in. I loved Sunday evenings because we always made a point to sit around the table and talk about each other's days, weeks, whatever. My mom and dad would always be drinking their coffee, Ben had his lemonade, and I had my iced tea. When it was my turn, I shared how excited I was to go to school the next day and tell Amy and Max all about our move. Ben rolled his eyes, disgusted—he was cashing in on his get-out-of-jail-free card. As we all began to talk about plans for the coming week, I stared at the black skyline of the woods against the evening sky. I thought about the doll and wondered if she belonged to a little girl who used to live in this house. If so, she had a story . . . everyone has a story.

4

My Besties, Amy and Max

My alarm buzzed at 6:30 a.m. Good Lord, I did not miss that sound! I smacked the snooze button and, though my body was telling me to do otherwise, forced myself to get up and out of bed. I gasped as my bare feet touched the floor. Damn wooden floors—since we'd moved in, I'd tried to accustom myself to the cold rush. My socks always fell off in my sleep, and I was too lazy to hunt for them under the covers when I woke up. I only had myself to blame for having not bought slippers yet.

The bus picked me up at 7:30, so that left more than enough time to get ready. My mom and dad were in the kitchen when I came down—she was drinking coffee and reading the morning paper and he was making pancakes. After enjoying a successful marketing career for many years, my mom had decided to make a change and work from home, offering marketing consulting services on a freelance basis. When my dad got his big bonus last year, the time seemed right for a shift. And she was happy. We'd been worried about how it would affect her, but she welcomed the change. And when Ben or I were home sick, she appreciated the flexibility of being able to take care of us.

Fresh pancakes were flopped on my plate as I sat down, with warm steam dancing upward.

"What's the occasion, Dad?"

"Well, we figured Ben shouldn't be the *only* one getting flapjacks this morning."

He smiled as he took another sip of coffee. I laughed when I saw the baby pancake on top. Since I was a little girl, my dad had always made me one little "baby" pancake to go with the rest. It was small, the size of a large button. Just one of those funny little father-daughter quirks we shared.

"Thanks, Dad." I smiled as I wolfed breakfast down.

I needed to eat fast because the bus would be here any second. I glanced at the clock—7:15.

"Thanks again for breakfast. I needed that!"

"You got it." My dad tipped his coffee mug my way.

"Well, I'm off. See you guys later!"

My mom put the paper down for a second. "Okay, have fun today! And tell Amy and Max we say hi."

"Thanks, I will!"

I grabbed my backpack and rushed out the door. Normally, I took my mornings much slower—but today was different from other mornings. I had questions that needed answers, and I was sure my friends could help. As the bus pulled to a stop at the corner of Belmont Avenue and Wicker Grove, my heart leaped and a smile spread across my face when I thought of seeing Amy and Max soon. Usually, we saw each other at least once on the weekends; but because of the move, I hadn't had the time.

Amy had actually offered to help me on Saturday, which my parents had said was completely fine, but her mom said she couldn't skip out on their family reunion. She had a very big family, much bigger than both Max's and mine combined. So family reunions were always important events, and not to be missed under any circumstances. Our family reunions were much smaller gatherings, and guests fluctuated year after year with children moving away and new generations being born. *C'est la vie* . . . The future was unpredictable, but as for the present, we were the closest of friends and wanted to keep it that way.

As the bus pulled up to our school, I lugged my backpack onto my shoulders and walked through the front doors. I loved where my locker was—a straight shot through the front doors, right next to my homeroom. Miss Peterson was my homeroom teacher, and she was very sweet. My last name was Kierney, Amy's was Diaz, and Max's was Walsh—so, unfortunately, we were all in different homerooms. Max and I were in the same biology class this year, though. And Amy, Max, and I were all in the same English class. English was also the last class of the day, so it was always nice to leave together after class and make plans for later on.

I stuffed my gear into my locker, gathered my books for history (my first class of the day), and headed to homeroom. I smiled at Miss Peterson as I walked in, and she smiled back above the papers she was grading. I hoped I'd eventually have her for one of my classes. She taught honors chemistry, though, and chemistry was neither a strong suit of mine nor a subject I was very passionate about. I would, most likely, take basic chemistry and have Mr. Cowell. I did hear he let his students take their tests home, though, so maybe I'd actually have a chance at getting an A in chemistry. Imagine that!

My expression turned to disgust as I walked to my seat next to one of the biggest jocks in school, Matt Kingston. He got by on his good looks and throwing arm. What had the world come to . . . He winked at me and grinned, revealing his toilet bowl-white teeth. His parents had tons of money, and unfortunately, this fueled his vanity. The most annoying thing, too, was as time went on, his vanity seemed to keep growing. Yet no one could see who he really was except for me and my friends and . . . well, any intellectual, really.

He now lived a few houses down from me, and his house stuck out like a big gaudy diamond. It was massive, complete with luxury cars parked in the driveway and meticulous landscaping. His mom came from money, which seemed to have helped his dad create his booming real estate business. And though his parents were rumored to be nice enough, he and his older sister were anything but. They supposedly had wild parties almost every weekend in the summer, which meant that mass stupidity would be wafting over to my house on the apologetic summer breeze. Lucky me!

This was usually the very first personal encounter I had every Monday, aside from the exchange of a smile and occasional greeting with Miss Peterson. I would amuse myself with thoughts of Matt working as a cheap salesman at some crappy retail store after graduating high school and knocking up his girlfriend, Kristy Meyers. Why were girls like her always ending up with guys like him? Sure, she was the head cheerleader, but she was *smart*. And you couldn't say that for most of the cheerleading team here at Westmont.

As for me, I wasn't dating anyone—yet. I'd had a couple boyfriends before, but our relationships (if you could call them that) were petty and brief. I needed intellect and wit, and they'd been . . . bland. Lately, though, I had my eyes on Josh Potter. He'd moved here last year and was a junior. Everything about him was perfect—tall, dark hair, brown eyes, a smile that could light up a room . . . *and* he was smart. In fact, I'd heard he was in a few honors classes. We'd flirted in the hallways before. I even dropped my books in front of him once so he'd help me pick them up! For shame . . . But those eyes and that smile—I could gaze at that face all day. Just then, the bell rang. I jumped in my seat, frazzled. Daydreaming again in homeroom—guilty as charged.

After homeroom, I headed to history class. After that, it was art and then lunch. After lunch, I had biology (with Max) and then Spanish. I didn't like my morning classes much because none of my friends were in them. I mean, I knew Sally Hirsch in history and Megan Pierce in art. Sally had a new boyfriend, it seemed, every week; and Megan was really into morbid, artsy dead poet stuff. She used art class as an outlet for this, and so a lot of times she'd paint dark and ominous pictures that usually had something to do with death. I really didn't understand it, but I guess to each their own. I liked dark and scary, but sometimes she took it too far.

This morning, Sally talked to me about how much fun she had with Bobby Ricker over the weekend. They'd been dating for about a week, but he had "rocked her world" Friday night. Megan talked about how she read Edgar Allan Poe over the weekend, and how "badass" Van Gogh was for cutting off his ear.

"Really? You're crazy. I wouldn't cut off my ear—or anything else—for *anyone*."

"That's what you say *now*. Have you ever been in love?"

"Pfft, no! And I sure as hell wouldn't cut my ear off if I was?!"

"Love can happen at any time, you know, with anyone."

She always caught me off guard, but I kinda liked that quirkiness about her.

"Okay, you're creepin' me out."

"How about Josh Potter?" She shot me a wink.

"What? No! I am not in *love* with Josh Potter."

"Well, maybe he's in love with *you*."

"Please . . ." We did flirt, but I bet he flirted with lots of girls.

"I just saw him checkin' you out when you walked in here. I don't know about you two." She looked down and drew a heart in her notebook.

"You're lying—Josh wasn't checking me out. There's plenty of other girls in this school who are prettier than me. Josh could have whoever he wants. Plus, what would he want with a freshman?"

"Don't sell yourself short. Katie Morris, Alison Knowles . . ." she began naming off cheerleaders' names, resting her chin on her palm and looking ahead. Then she turned toward me. "Yeah, you're right. I'd take petty and dramatic over smart and sophisticated any day."

I snickered. *"You* know what I *mean*."

"I don't, really—enlighten me."

"Nothing. It's . . . it doesn't even matter. I have no chance with Josh."

"Suit yourself, but I'll have to disagree with you on that one."

I felt saved when the bell rang—I grabbed my lunch from my locker and headed down to the cafeteria. As I entered the glass doors to the lunchroom, I looked toward the back of the room at the table we had all designated as "ours" at the beginning of the school year. We liked it because it was all the way in the back by the windows and when we wanted to, we could snicker at the stoners playing with their hacky sacks and the boring popular kids. Amy and Max were already sitting there, getting their lunches out and laughing about something. They always put a smile on my face when I really needed one.

"What is up?!" I slid next to Max.

"Jess! It feels like we haven't seen each other in like a month or something!" Max blurted out. Her blue eyes sparkled against her jet-black hair.

"I know, doesn't it?" Amy agreed. "I mean, really, I couldn't wait to see you guys today. It's one of those weird days when I *actually* want to come to school."

"I know! I'm the same way. This weekend just felt so long. We didn't see each other, talk on the phone—nothing! Never again, guys. Now that I'm off the grid, I need you so that I don't go insane." Grasping my head in my hands, I cringed and looked at the ceiling. "Okay, well, it's not *that* bad. Just a new location and kind of too far from any civilization. I can deal, though."

"Aww, it'll be cool, Jess. In fact, Max and I were just talking about this weekend."

Amy took a sip of bottled water before continuing. "We wanna come visit—spend the night, maybe? It'll be fun!"

"That sounds awesome! I'd love to have you guys over. It's huge! A lot bigger than our old house. A little creepy in some ways, but I guess that comes with an old house and all."

Max went on to talk about her weekend; she'd helped her mom grade papers on Saturday (her mom taught first grade) and then practiced for track. She was one of the best sprinters on the team. On Sunday, she did some homework and spring cleaning—her room was usually a minefield. "Pretty uneventful weekend."

Amy talked about their family reunion, and about how every year her aunts and uncles would just look at her and tell her what a beautiful young woman she was becoming. Amy hated this because even though she knew they meant it as a compliment, she was very self-conscious about her body. She was more developed than either Max and I, and always made it a point to try to cover up as much as possible. While there were so many girls who would do anything to have Amy's figure, she'd happily switch places with them. I didn't get it, but then again, I didn't get teased like she did. Though it was annoying now, Max and I kept telling her when she got older, she'd be a hottie and would stop men dead in their tracks. Amy always blushed and shyly thanked us. She was more mature than Max and I, but we loved this about her. Her traits definitely balanced out Max's ridiculous humor and my daydreaming tendencies.

Before lunch ended, we talked again about the coming weekend and plans for a sleepover at my new house. I told them I'd ask my parents and call them tonight about it. I was so excited and couldn't wait to show them our new place. And maybe, depending on how this week went, I'd even be brave enough to explore the room up by the attic. I didn't know if I had the courage to go up there alone, but if Amy and Max were with me, I'd feel safer. The second they mentioned a sleepover, the idea popped into my head. When lunch was over, we threw our brown bags in the garbage and headed together down the hall.

Amy's locker was closest to the lunchroom. "Well, see you guys in English! Big day—*The Crucible*. Gives me the shivers!" she said as she walked to her locker, cringing.

We were going to start reading this play today. Our English teacher, Mrs. Rosen, mentioned it last week. All three of us, being avid readers in general, were fascinated by the topic of witchcraft.

"What are we doing in biology today?" Max asked.

"Ya know, I have absolutely *no* idea. For all I know, we could be having a quiz."

"Not funny, Jess." She frowned. "Seriously, though, you know I'm behind in that class! You better be lying, or else you'll be dissecting a little froggy next week all by yourself."

"Eww, gross!" I paused. "Well, hey—we're in this together, my friend. You gotta get your hands dirty just as much as I do. I'll see ya there, goof," nudging her with my shoulder.

"See ya . . ." Max walked to her locker, which, to her disdain, was nowhere near any of her classes. As it turned out, there actually was a surprise quiz in biology today. Luckily, I'd been keeping up with my reading, so I was confident I answered a good majority of the questions correctly. From the look on Max's face, I gathered quite the opposite. She was tapping her pencil on her desk in a steady rhythm and biting her lower lip. I handed my quiz in to Mr. Hendricks, nodded a "see ya" to Max, and headed out the door. She just shook her head and mouthed "you suck," her usual parting message when I left biology after a quiz or test day—she almost never left before me.

Mr. Hendricks always let his students leave class after they were done with their quizzes and tests, which was a blessing to me this year because I was struggling in Spanish lately. I took the extra time I had in between classes to get to Mrs. Lopez's classroom early and read up on the material beforehand. I had no friends in Spanish class, which was fine with me because I was really trying hard to get a good grade. Matt Kingston's girlfriend Kristy Meyers was in the class, though. And every day, I had to endure listening to her carry on a conversation with one of her cheerleader friends who was not so intellectually gifted. Today her friend was dramatically elaborating on why she needed to lose at least five pounds by next Friday for their game against the Montville Tigers. I rolled my eyes and waited for class to start.

Spanish class actually went by like a breeze. Thankfully, there was no surprise Monday quiz, and we just brushed up on what we had gone over last Friday. I gathered up my books, made a pit stop at my locker, and walked briskly to Mrs. Rosen's room. As I entered, she was placing reading material on each of our desks.

"Hi, Mrs. Rosen, how was your weekend?"

"Oh, it was very nice, Jess. Thanks for asking. I took my daughter to the zoo on Sunday—gained some nice mommy points for that one." We both chuckled as I sat down. I really liked Mrs. Rosen. She was in her early thirties with beautiful long black curly hair and a smile that just lit up the room. Not only was English my favorite subject, but I also loved her personality and how passionate she was about teaching.

"Hey, Jess!" Max came rushing into the room and almost knocked me off my chair, swinging her backpack off her shoulders.

"Why do you carry that thing around all day? It's like a bag of *rocks!*"

"Hey, serious people take serious measures. And I'm serious about *learning*, that's no lie. In fact, jot that one down for a rainy day. Maybe it'll come in handy sometime."

"Max, you never cease to amaze me," Mrs. Rosen remarked as she shot a quick glance and a smile at Max.

"Thanks, Mrs. Rosen. I will take that as a compliment." She winked, tipping her head to Mrs. Rosen and grinning from ear to ear. Leaning back, she crossed her arms as if to congratulate herself on a job well done.

"You're crazy, Max," I said. She really was the joker of our little group. I was the dreamer, Max was the joker, and Amy—well, since she was the most mature, we liked to bust her chops from time to time. Amy breezed in just seconds later, her beautiful caramel hair pulled into a perfect ponytail and books stacked from largest to smallest. She always carried her daily planner on top, textbooks in the middle, and notebooks on the bottom. This never changed. Sometimes Max and I would flip them around when she wasn't looking and she'd sneer and quickly change them back, usually muttering something like, "You guys . . .I swear . . ." She sat at the desk behind me, and Max had the desk next to me.

"Hey Ames, how's it shakin'?" Max turned around to face us both.

"Oh, it's all right. I had two surprise quizzes today—biology and history. So that kinda sucked, but I'm pretty sure I passed them both."

"Yeah, I think Miss Max here bombed her biology quiz this afternoon." I glanced at Max.

"Ha, really funny Miss *No hablo Espanol*," Max quipped. I sneered back at her. I sucked at Spanish and Max sucked at biology. "Seriously, though, I *did* pretty much bomb that quiz. I hate biology—remind me never to, like, consider a career in that stuff."

We all laughed. Just then, Mrs. Rosen asked for the class to be quiet and turn to the first page of the play. She gave us a brief summary of the author's life and works, then delved into a discussion about the topic. I was fascinated with the subject matter—witches and evil spirits. Although it left much to the imagination, I felt there *had* to be some truth to it.

5

Vivid Nightmare

As class ended, Max, Amy, and I gathered up our books and talked about heading over to Christie's Cafe for some ice cream—they made the best sundaes. Unless one of us had to go home early, Mondays after school were always designated Christie's days. We'd chat over sundaes (I always had vanilla topped with caramel, Amy had strawberry, and Max had chocolate) and our moms would pick us up around 5:00.

"Oh, man. I swear, all I could think about today was this chocolate sundae. Screw school, I need my chocolate!" Max scooped up a huge spoonful of gooey chocolate and savored the taste, closing her eyes and smiling.

"Yeah, I didn't have like *anything* sweet this weekend, so this is a real treat for me. I'm trying to cut down on sugar and stuff because it's going straight to my hips." Amy glanced down at her waist.

"Amy, you look *great*. What are you *talking* about? And, for God's sake, we're fifteen! Our metabolism is still sky high. You shouldn't start worrying about what you eat until you're like forty! That's when stuff starts to show, or so I've read." Even though I wasn't nearly as self-conscious about my weight as Amy was, I did find myself reading about health stuff now and then in magazines. One thing they always seemed to mention was that when a woman hits forty, metabolism takes a nosedive.

"Thanks, Jess. I wish I were like you that way. It would be so nice to have a day where I wasn't thinking about how what I eat is gonna look like on my hips." She sat back, sighed, and stared at the ceiling.

"Your hips are *perfect*, Ames. Hell, *you* are perfect! I mean, look at me—I'm tall and thin, but boobs? What the hell are those?" Max cocked her head, looking at us questionably and pointing to her chest. Unlike Amy, she didn't have much. She didn't care, though, and that's what I loved about her. Max was one of the lucky ones when it came to food. She could eat whatever she wanted, as often as she wanted, and it never seemed to matter. Plus, at 5'8", she was taller than Amy and me (we both stood about 5'4"), so things just sort of seemed to distribute evenly on her slim figure.

I ate another spoonful of ice cream, and decided it was the right time to ask them about Wicker Grove. "So, do you guys remember when I told you about the new house we were moving to?"

Amy and Max paused for a second, glanced awkwardly at each other, and then went on eating.

"Yeah," Max said. "Why, what's up?"

"Well, I just remember when I told you guys, you just kinda . . . it's like this look shot over both your faces. Like you knew something, but you didn't want to say it."

"Well," Amy swirled circles in her ice cream with her spoon. "I mean, it's just that, we've heard stories and stuff about that house. The family that used to live there, I mean . . . I don't know who they were or anything . . . but after they moved out no one wanted to buy it."

"Until your parents took a liking to it," Max continued.

"Why did your parents want to buy *that* house?" Amy asked.

"What do you mean, *that* house?"

"Well, it's just that—out of all the houses they could have bought, why *that* one?"

"Well, my mom and dad were looking around for a while. They knew what they wanted—larger house, more rooms, bigger backyard. Just more space and stuff. Plus, my dad finally has room to store his woodwork and their bedroom is ginormous. Ben and I both have bigger rooms, and then . . . Well, then there's the attic and stuff, which is supposed to be pretty big." Max and Amy were both staring at me. They knew I wasn't done, and they were right—I wasn't. "And there's the room up by the attic." I glanced at them from beneath my brow, feeling as though I were being interrogated.

"Yeah, that room," Max said.

"What do you guys know . . . honestly? C'mon! I *know* you know *something*." I twirled my finger in their faces as if I were hypnotizing them.

"Well, I can tell you what I . . . what *we* know," Max said, glancing at Amy. "I mean, it's just rumors, but apparently some kind of voodoo stuff used to happen in that room. Before the Crawfords moved in, I mean. That was the name of the family. A lady lived there before they did . . . she lived there alone. And she wasn't someone you wanted to cross, if you get my drift. Apparently she'd lived there for a *very* long time. And no one really knows what happened to her. She just . . . disappeared."

My skin prickled and I suddenly felt squeamish, like spiders were crawling all over me.

"You okay?" Amy's facial expression was that of concern and guilt.

Leaning back, arms out, I said, "Yeah, I'm fine, guys. You just told me some voodoo shit went down in my house, but I'm okay."

"What, you want us to *lie* to you?!"

"*No*, Max. Just . . . this is messed up. Just give me a second. Crawford . . ."

"What's wrong?" Max asked.

"I'm fine! I mean, not *fine*. I just . . . I guess it's just nice to finally have a name for them, ya know? This whole time, I knew nothing about the family . . . Did they have a little girl?"

"They did. She was about ten years old when they moved in," Amy said. "I think her name was Hannah."

"Hannah . . . Hannah Crawford," I repeated, staring off into space. *That doll . . . why would a ten-year-old still be carrying around a doll?*

"You okay, Jess?" Amy interrupted my thoughts.

"Yeah, you okay? You look like you're about to fall into some kind of deep trance. Jessica, Jessica, Jessica . . ." Max repeated slowly as she waved her hand in front of my face.

"Cut it out, *Maxine*!"

"Oh no you *didn't* . . ." Max leaned back, hands still on the table, and sneered at me. She hated being called Maxine. "*Sorry*, Jess. Just tryin' to see if you're still *among* us."

"No, I'm sorry . . . I'm just thinking about this doll I found in our backyard."

"*What* doll?" Amy asked as her green eyes widened with curiosity.

I started to tell them about the little patch of pine trees in the backyard by the forest, and about the perfect little doll I'd found on the ground. They both listened to me wide-eyed, mouths half open in awe.

"Now *that's* freaky," Amy said.

"Well, *yeah*. And for all we know, that could have been like a voodoo doll or something. I mean, what the hell?"

"Well . . . that's not even the worst part. Hannah disappeared about a year ago," Max said.

"*Disappeared?* What do you mean? Where'd she go?" Then, slamming my hands on the table, "She disappeared . . . from our house?!"

"Jess, c'mon. We're, like, in the middle of a restaurant."

"Sorry, Max. I'm just a little *frazzled* here . . . and I kinda feel, like, not on solid ground. If she disappeared, did something happen in that house?" My voice quieted to a whisper, "Did she, like, get murdered or something?" Then, "Wait, I remember hearing about this . . . I remember when this girl went missing. How could that have been *our* house? Of all the houses we looked at . . ."

"Jess, c'mon. Seriously, calm down." Max laughed nervously, looking around us.

"I mean, no one really knows what happened. All I know is her parents went to check on her one day and she was gone. Not in her room, not in the yard, nowhere. Just, *gone* . . ." Amy said.

"I don't understand," shaking my head. "Maybe someone *kidnapped* her?"

"No one has been able to prove anything," Amy said. "And there was no evidence of foul play. It's a mystery."

"Oh my God." I leaned on the table with my head in my hands.

"Jess—that was, like, over a year ago. Maybe even more. And nothing bad has happened since. You're fine." Max shot

Amy a look of concern as she said this. "The Crawfords apparently moved out a few months after Hannah went missing, somewhere close by. So the house was on the market since then. I don't think they could bear to live there anymore."

"I don't like this, guys. I don't like this *one bit*. A year is not a long time. That house *definitely* has bad vibes sometimes. I've even been having these horrible nightmares since we moved in."

"Jess," Amy pleaded. "*C'mon*, you'll be *fine*. It's just a new house and a big change for you, and you're working yourself up for nothing. Max and I will come over this weekend. We'll have a sleepover—it'll be fun! That'll take your mind off all this." She tilted her head and smiled at me, dimples in full form. She looked so cute when she did this, I couldn't help but smile back.

"Thanks, Amy." I ran my hands through my hair, absentmindedly noticing how soft it was. "Yeah, hopefully you guys can come over. I don't think we have anything going on . . . And maybe I'm overreacting. But still, this is scary shit! Why the hell did my parents have to buy *this* house? And how could they not have *known* about this?"

"Ain't *that* the truth," Max chimed in. "I mean, who knows? I think someone may have actually died in our house because whenever I want a swig of orange juice it's all gone. Now *somebody* has to drink that orange juice . . ." She attempted a serious look but failed. "Okay, just kidding, I don't know where that was going, except it was going nowhere . . ."

"What?!" I laughed.

"Just trying to lighten the mood," Max shrugged.

Just then, my mom walked through the door.

"Well, gotta go," I said. "I'll see you guys tomorrow. Even though what you both said still freaks me out, whatever—I can deal. At least *I'm* still here!" We all exchanged an awkward laugh with each other.

"Yeah, let's not joke about that," Max said. "I mean, we all know nothing's going to happen to you and you won't go missing but, still—you're our *girl*!" We all hugged each other goodbye, then I walked over to my mom.

"Thanks for picking me up, Mom."

"Of *course*. I know how much your Mondays mean to you with the girls. Is there room in there for dinner?" She pointed at my stomach.

"Oh, yeah—I didn't eat much, really. Funny how on Mondays I always switch it up. First dessert, then dinner."

"And sometimes more dessert after dinner!"

"Yes, I must admit, I am guilty of that from time to time." I grinned and patted my belly.

I told her about my day as we drove home. Then, I switched the topic. "Hey, so we had kind of an interesting talk at Christie's." I looked at her from the corner of my eye.

"Oh yeah? What'd you guys talk about?"

"Well, I asked them some questions about the house and stuff."

"And . . .?"

"Well, mostly, I just wanted to know more about the family, you know? The family that lived there before we moved in."

"Okay. What'd you find out?"

"Well, they had a daughter."

"I don't know anything about the family that lived there before us. But maybe that was their daughter's doll that you found out back then?"

"Well, did you know their daughter disappeared about a year ago?"

My mom was quiet. Then, glancing at me, "Is that what Amy

and Max told you?"

"Yeah . . . You didn't know?"

"I knew this house had been on sale for a few months before we put in an offer. But no . . . oh, Jess. But I remember now. I remember, about a year ago, hearing about that little girl. No, I didn't know this . . . I wonder what . . ."

"How could you not know it happened in our *house*?!" I stretched out my arms accusingly.

She shot me a cold look.

"Sorry, sorry . . . Didn't mean to yell. But still . . . how??"

"Jess . . . this is horrible. It's . . . *shocking* to me. But we don't know the details here."

"Well, this is just great. Thanks a lot. *Really.*"

Her face grew stern. "I know how your mind works. You can scare yourself to pieces with your own imagination. Like I said, we don't know the details. For all we know, their daughter has been found and they have moved on to their new chapter in their new house."

Frustrated, I folded my arms and stared straight ahead. We were almost home, I could see the road curve off to Wicker Grove in the distance. It was raining and the street signs glistened in the shine of the headlights.

"Thanks, Mom. I . . . I appreciate you trying to help here. But if their daughter was found, wouldn't we have heard about it?"

"Yes, I suppose so . . ."

"I just wish I would have known this . . ."

"Why? So you could wake up in a cold sweat every night?!"

"No, it's just—it's the truth, right? I just want to know the truth, that's all. It's disturbing, but . . ." Suddenly, my expression froze and my jawed dropped.

"Jess, what on earth is it?"

I turned to her. "What room was hers? Mom, which room? Mine or Ben's?"

"Jess, how could I *know* that?" She pulled the car to a stop in front of our house, and in the silence, all I could hear was the soothing patter of rain on the roof.

"Well, what if it was *my* room?"

"Jess . . ." She softly ran her fingers through my hair. I loved when she did that. "Listen. We just moved. I did *not* know about this. Obviously, if I did, we would have moved somewhere different. It's devastating. But . . . it's something we have to come to grips with now."

"Okay, I'm sorry. I'm just—I get obsessed about stuff, you know." I slapped my hands on my knees. "Of *course* you know that! You're my mom, it's your *job!*"

"That's right. And I *also* know you have nothing to worry about. Stuff like this, it's horrible. It's *really* horrible, but sometimes it happens. And, like I said . . . it's the *details*. You can't fester in this. May that poor family find peace, and may they find their little girl."

All I'll be doing is festering. "You're right," I said, nodding. "I've been *cleansed* of the evil thoughts plaguing me!"

"There goes your *imagination* again. C'mon, let's go."

Ben was on the couch watching TV in the den when we walked in. Slapping the back of his head, I chimed, "Hey Benny!"

"Jess, c'mon! *Don't!*"

"That's what big sisters are for—rough you up a bit."

"Whatever . . ." he mumbled.

"Hi Dad," He was busy at work in his office.

"Hi, hun! How was your day?"

Trying to shake off the conversation I'd just had, "Oh, it was good. I had a pop quiz in biology, but I think I did pretty good.

Can't say the same for Max, though."

"Oh, that's too bad. You guys should really study together more. You know, you can help her with biology and she can help you with Spanish."

"I know. Max and Amy want to come over this weekend for a sleepover. I haven't asked Mom yet, but is that cool?"

"Oh, yeah, sure—that's fine. Just run it by Mom, but I don't think we have anything going on."

"Okay, thanks!"

After my mom told me my friends could come over, I walked into my room and closed the door behind me. Throwing my backpack on the floor, I fell onto my bed. The bedding was so soft, and for some reason, it felt even softer when I came home than when I went to bed at night. I changed my clothes, threw on my comfy hoodie and sweatpants, and headed downstairs. My mom already had dinner going, so I plopped down on the couch in the living room and turned on the TV, hoping to catch some *Unsolved Mysteries* reruns.

"So how was your day, Ben?"

"All right," he called from the den. "I mean, I didn't do that much, just chilled out most of the day."

"Yeah, I figured . . ."

No luck finding reruns today, and nothing good was on either.

"Dinner's ready!" my mom called from the kitchen, putting an end to my endless scrolling. Ben and I stumbled into the kitchen and we all enjoyed another delicious dinner together—pork chops, broccoli, and mashed potatoes. I welcomed the distraction from my racing thoughts, and I was sure my mom did too after our conversation. Sometimes it seemed there was a hamster in my head incessantly spinning his wheel.

I couldn't sleep that night. I knew I wasn't going to be able to the second Amy and Max told me about the Crawford girl. Hannah Crawford . . . I repeated her name over and over in my head. Then came the nightmares . . . horrible visions that had haunted me for the last few nights. Restless, I pulled the comforter over my head and could feel the sweat already soaking the sheets.

Hannah was sitting in a rocking chair in the corner of my room. She had beautiful black hair that flowed down to her waist, and its brilliant sheen glistened in the moonlight pouring in through the window. She wore a baby blue dress with a high lacy collar and short puffy sleeves, just like the doll I'd found in the yard. She wore white stockings and her shoes were black Mary Janes. She rocked back and forth slowly in the chair, staring at me with dark eyes wide open.

I squeezed my eyes tighter, trying to block her out. Rainbows, unicorns, green pastures—they flickered in my mind vividly and then were gone. And there she was again—motionless with her head cocked, and eyes fixed on me. Slowly she walked toward my bed, her gait uneasy and off balance like a zombie's. Her sad eyes drooped with despair, and dried tears shimmered on her cheeks in the moonlight. Then she was standing next to me, facing my bed. Slowly, her gaze lowered as she stared down at me, fearfully wrapped tight in my comforter. Her cherub face was more visible now, and her eyes were calling to me. She was terrifying, but at the same time, fragile and vulnerable. Her skin was pale, the shade of death. One arm dangled at her side, and her small fingers hung lifeless. She tilted her head, and her arm lifted slowly . . . ever so slowly. Hand outstretched, she reached for the comforter, her fingers seeking the soft fabric . .
.

42

I shot out of bed—literally jumping onto the floor and swinging my arms anywhere and everywhere with my eyes closed. I didn't dare open them, fearful of what I might see. Finally mustering the courage to open my eyes, I ran to the light switch. I turned it on and, breathing heavily and doused in sweat, leaned my back against the wall. There was no Hannah and there was no rocking chair. The whole house was silent, and I felt small and insignificant in its mass. I slept with my light on for the rest of the night.

6

A Plan Is Made

The next morning, I could hardly stay awake for breakfast. I barely kept my eyes open, and the fact that it was only Tuesday made me even less motivated for the rest of the school week.

"Jess, you okay? You look like you're about to give yourself an oatmeal face mask." My mom's voice sounded far away even though she was standing right next to me. I suddenly jerked my head up, realizing I was just inches from my bowl of oatmeal.

"Oh, yeah. I'm fine, Mom. I just . . . I just had a hard time sleeping last night, that's all. I guess I'm still getting used to my new room, ya know?" I shot her a sleepy smile, trying my best to mask the lie.

"You weren't giving yourself nightmares again, were you? About last night?"

"What are you guys talking about?" Ben was staring at us from the fridge.

"Oh, nothing—just mom and daughter stuff. You know, all that mushy girly stuff." My mom smirked.

"Yeah, that would give me nightmares too."

My mom and I looked at each other and laughed. Ben just

44

stared at us, his expression that of naive confusion.

"What's so funny? I'm serious!"

We burst out laughing.

"Whatever . . ." He grabbed his empty bowl, put it in the sink, and headed up to his room. Seemed he had a case of the morning grumpies.

"Ben, you need to be ready soon!" my mom called up after him.

"Yeah, Mom, I just gotta get my books. Plus, I wanted to get away from Jess."

"Nice—I love you too!" I chimed sweetly. Then, turning to my mom, "Okay, I wasn't completely honest with you about last night."

"I'm listening." She sat down next to me, leaning her head on her hand and giving me her full attention. *I love you, Mom.*

"So, just hearing about that little girl, Hannah, and how she disappeared from this house and . . . I just had really bad nightmares. I had to sleep with the light on all night."

"Oh, Jess . . ." She ran her fingers through my hair again. "It's okay. And no one's gonna hurt you. There are no ghosts, no spirits . . ." She could sense my unease. "Okay, easier said than done. Just try not to let this get to you too much."

"I know, I know." I rested my head in my hands. "It's just, I had this horrible nightmare last night that she—Hannah—was in this rocking chair in my room, and she was just staring at me. She looked like a normal little girl. I remember it clear as day. She had this blue dress on, and these white stockings and black shoes. And her hair was long and dark . . . beautiful long hair. It felt so real. I was so scared, I didn't want to open my eyes."

"Well, hey, if you have to sleep with your light on for a week, a month, a year—so be it."

"Thanks, Mom. Really, thanks so much for listening to me. I was scared to tell you because I feel . . . well . . . like, weak or something. It's stupid. I just . . . *you* know." I pointed to my head. "My mind is my worst enemy."

"It's okay, hun. And please, don't ever think that about yourself. In fact, I think you've been dealing with this pretty well. And these feelings will pass—they're just all in that precious little head of yours." She pressed the tip of her finger to my forehead. "May they find their little girl, and may she come home."

"Yes . . . And I know, I'll be fine. Thanks, Mom."

I glanced at the clock. "Oh, crap, the bus will be here any minute. Gotta go!"

"Tell your brother to hurry up—I don't know what's taking him so long."

"I'm here!" Ben trotted down the stairs.

"C'mon, let's go."

"Love you both! Have a good day!" My mom blew us a kiss.

"Love you too, Mom," I said.

"Yeah, love you!" Ben was walking slightly behind me, stuffing a textbook into his backpack. We headed to the bus stop together. Our middle school and high school were practically next to each other, so we took the same bus.

Unlike other brothers and sisters who preferred to sit in separate seats on the bus, Ben and I usually sat next to each other. Some days we didn't talk much—some not at all.

"Why you so tired, Jess?"

"Oh, I . . . I just . . . Like I told Mom, it's just the new house and all." I was leaning my elbow against the window, my forehead cradled in my palm. "It's really nothing. Not that big of a deal. I'll get over it." I smiled and messed up his hair a little with my fingers, a loving gesture that he couldn't stand. He glared at me, frowning with arms crossed. *Geez, if you don't want the attention, then don't ask.*

Ben suddenly broke the silence. "I've been having these dreams . . ."

"About what?"

"There's a girl—she tells me she needs help. I keep on having them . . ."

Fear gripped me and goose bumps popped up all over my arms.

"How long have you had these dreams for? And why didn't you *tell* me?"

"I don't know, they just started a few days ago. I didn't tell you because it's . . . *embarrassing.*"

"How is it *embarrassing?*"

Under his breath, he said, "Because I'm *scared*, Jess!"

"Ben, being scared doesn't mean you're weak or something. And hell, that would scare me *too.*" *Lying through my teeth—I'm already horrified.*

"She's like, wearing this blue dress. And she has long dark hair. She's younger than you, like my age."

Swallowing a huge gulp, I asked, "Does she tell you *why* she needs help?"

"She tells me something horrible happened to her, and she's stuck in our house."

What the . . .

I didn't even notice when Ben got up to walk off the bus as it pulled to a stop, but I vaguely remembered hearing him say my name.

"Girl, what is wrong with you? The bus has stopped. You're here. Now get your little butt off to school!" Our bus driver,

Mrs. Smith, was staring at me and tapping her fingernails on the steering wheel.

"Oh . . . sorry Mrs. Smith." I hadn't realized I was just standing in the aisle, spaced out, arms limply at my sides.

"That's all right, sweetie. Just get your butt movin'—don't want to be late."

"Thanks, bye!" I flashed her my best attempt at a smile, turned my head, and darted off to school. Head down, I contemplated my situation until I suddenly ran into somebody. *Oh, this is the last thing I need right now . . .*

"Jess, you okay?" Josh Potter was staring at me with his dreamy chocolate-brown eyes.

"Oh, I . . . I . . . Sorry!"

"What are you saying *sorry* for? It's not your fault. Here . . ." He picked up my things for me. This was the first time I ran into him on accident—go figure.

"Thanks, Josh," I curled my lips and flashed him a big smile. *Gotta get my flirt on while I can.*

"No problem. Hey, how's the new house holdin' up?"

"New house?"

"Yeah, your friend Max told me you just moved."

Jess! Dumb!

"Oh, yeah. *That* new house."

He stared at me, confused.

"Oh, it's nothing—just trying to be funny. But failing."

He smiled. *He was so cute!*

"It . . . it's really going good. All moved in and getting used to things, so it's cool. Thanks for asking."

"Good to hear. Well, sorry to cut it short, but I gotta head off to class. I'll see ya around?"

"Yeah, I'll see ya. Thanks, Josh."

I watched him walk away and sighed. He was perfect. I just couldn't bring myself to ever say anything meaningful to him—every time we ran into each other (even literally this time), I just kinda froze up. I liked him *a lot;* but lately, this whole Hannah thing had taken over. I wanted to get to the bottom of it, whatever it was.

After our morning classes, Amy, Max, and I talked at lunch about the general gossip going around school that day. Sally Hirsch and Bobby Ricker had apparently ended it last night when Sally dumped him for Jesse Mills. From what Max heard, Bobby had a real blowout with Sally before homeroom, and he told her off big time. He called her every name in the book, and she stormed off crying. I thought something was bothering her this morning when we were in history class, because all she said was a meek little, "Oh, hi," when I said hello to her. During class, she just leaned on her elbow, chin cupped in her hand, and scribbled in her notebook. Even though she tried to look tough on the exterior, I could tell there was a lonely, sad girl inside.

"Stupid, stupid girl." Max rolled her eyes.

"Aww, she's not *that* bad. I mean, yeah, she gets around. But she's a nice person."

"Yeah, nice and *easy.*"

"That's not nice, Max." I couldn't help giggling.

"Hey, the truth hurts, but *someone's* gotta say it. Might as well be me," she quipped.

"Man, Bobby must have really liked her. Usually, the guys she dates couldn't give two shits if she wants to call it quits. I mean, they both get what they want then move on. Whatever . . . I couldn't care less about guys at this point."

"Oh yeah? What about Josh Potter?" Max playfully elbowed

49

me in the side.

"Haha . . . *No.* Yes, I admit he's cute, and he's nice and all. But nothing's gonna happen."

"What do you *mean*, nothing's gonna happen? You never know, Jess. Besides, he asked about you when we ran into each other yesterday." Max smiled like she knew a secret she wasn't gonna tell me.

"I know, I bumped into him this morning. He told me."

"Bumped into him, ha! Let me guess . . . like, on *purpose*?"

"*No*, Max. This time it was actually an accident."

"I think something's gonna happen between you two. You'd be such a cute pair," Amy said.

"So much pressure, and we're not even dating. Lord help me if that ever happens!"

"Well, you guys aren't gettin' any younger. One of these days, something's bound to spark between ya," Max smirked.

"Maybe . . . maybe not. And maybe, *just* maybe . . . I'll keep it a secret!"

"Ahh! Not cool, Jess. We're your *besties*!" Amy put her arm around me.

"Yeah. Seriously, Jess, that's not funny. We need to know— this is important stuff here!" Max blurted out.

"Okay, okay, you guys got me. Of *course*, you will be the first to know of my romantic encounters . . . when they begin. Then I'll move into my giant Gothic castle filled with gargoyles and all things dark and kooky and cool—think *Edward Scissorhands*. And I'll have my tall, broody—and romantic and handsome— man beside me. But I'm warning you, I don't know when that will be. So hold your horses."

"You're such a weirdo. But *Edward Scissorhands*, that's cool," Max said.

After a pause, I asked, "What the hell's going on with *Matt Kingston?*" I'd been bothered by it, and no one seemed to notice or care.

Max and Amy were confused.

"Where'd *that* come from?" Amy asked.

"I don't know . . . star football player, wrestler of the year . . . he's even acing tests lately. Scoring up there with the really smart kids. Just doesn't make sense. That should be the smart, broody ones. Not *him.*"

"His parents are probably bribing the school or something," Max jeered.

"Yeah, I wouldn't be surprised," Amy chimed in.

"But why should all this stuff happen to someone like *him?*"

"I don't know, Jess. But whatever it is, I also don't *care.*"

"Yeah, you're right, Ames. Who cares. Besides, karma's a bitch. And he's more than due his."

We raised our water bottles in a toast to not caring. And as we did, I remembered they were sleeping over on Friday night, and I'd made up my mind this morning about what I wanted to do. I needed to find out what was in that room, and Amy and Max were coming with me.

The week sped along, and I was grateful there were no more surprise quizzes or scheduled tests. It was hard to absorb any textbook information lately because every day I was consumed with thoughts about that little girl. My homework had taken a back seat, and I began to slack off. I caught up on my studies here and there when I had time—the bus ride home, after dinner—but most often, in the wee hours of the morning in my bedroom. I still slept with the light on, and my nightmares had finally subsided. I still dreamed of Hannah, but the dreams were different now.

Most of the time she was in the backyard, her baby blue dress falling around her. She was running and laughing, twirling in circles, her cherub face turned up to the sky. The sunlight bathed her little pink nose and rosy cheeks, and I could almost feel the soft warmth of the sun on her skin. Then someone called from behind her. She turned around and there was an older lady standing on the deck, beckoning her to come inside. The sunlight faded, and the sky turned gray. The warm summer breeze turned frigid and it chilled her skin. Her smile faded, and a look of fear spread across her face as she stared at the lady in the distance. Standing still, her hair writhed in the wind and her dress violently whipped back and forth. Even so, she stood firm. Then her mouth opened, and from the heavens, rain came crashing down to the earth. And then she was gone—it always ended the same. The storm came and washed her away.

I woke up Friday morning with a mission. Tonight was the night. We were going up that hallway, God help us. The thought frightened the hell out of me, but there was no turning back. It was like an open wound that wouldn't heal, and it was consuming me. I opened up my bedroom door and looked across the hallway. Ben's door was closed. I wondered how much he'd slept last night. Raising my hand to knock on his door, I thought otherwise. We'd see each other eventually this morning, and I didn't want to wake him.

As I got out of the shower, the mouthwatering scent of pancakes wafted upstairs. I closed my eyes, took a deep breath in, and savored the delicious smell. My dad looked up at me from the bottom of the stairs. "You *know*, kiddo, they taste even better than they smell."

"Hey, it's too early to joke around. I don't have any comebacks!"

He let out a hearty laugh. "You gotta be nice to the old man, you know. That's why I catch you off guard with these early in the morning. I know I'm safe from those Jess jabs."

I let out a yawn. "Did you make the baby pancake?"

"Yep, two this morning. Because it's Friday."

I walked down the stairs, and there on a plate were my two baby pancakes next to the big ones. I smiled from ear to ear. My mom was in the living room watching a morning show.

"Hey, Mom."

"Hi, hun. How'd you sleep?"

"Oh, all right. I'm just happy it's Friday. It's been a long week."

"Yeah, well, add on moving to a new place and you got yourself one hell of a week."

"Definitely."

"I know what'll put you in a better mood, though." She smiled as she casually flipped channels while I waited for her to continue.

"What?"

"Pizza! Why don't we have a pizza tonight? It's Friday!"

My mom knew that no matter how bad my Friday morning might be and how I dreaded the rest of the day, the thought of coming home and eating some steaming hot pepperoni pizza always put a smile on my face.

"Oh, man. Pepperoni pizza is calling my name! Wait, *double* pepperoni—make it double. You know what's lame?" I laughed. "I'll be thinking about pizza all day today."

"Well, make that *two* of us," she joked. "So, when are Max and Amy coming over? Are they riding home with you on the bus today?"

"Yeah, I think that's what they're planning."

"Okay, great."

Ben was already at the table scarfing down breakfast.

"When did *you* get downstairs, fart face?"

"I've been sitting here eating your pancakes while you and Mom were talking." He smiled and opened his mouth, showing me a bunch of half-eaten pancakes.

"Eww, Ben. That's gross!" *Brothers . . .*

We walked to the bus stop in silence that morning, kicking up dirt here and there. Ben and I hadn't talked about Hannah since our conversation Tuesday morning. For some odd reason, after he revealed that to me, I just felt further away from him. It was like he was superior in some way because she had actually spoken to him, even though it was in a dream.

"So, how'd you sleep last night?"

"Good," he said. "Why? You didn't?"

"Oh, no . . . I slept fine. I just thought that . . . well, maybe you had one of those dreams again? About the girl?"

"No, thank *God*." He picked up a stick and tapped it on the pavement as we walked.

"Weird . . ."

"What do you *mean*, weird? I was scared! Some girl stuck in our house . . ."

"Yeah, but . . . Do you think it's true?"

"Jess, don't do this. You and your freakin' horror movies . . ."

"What??"

"They were just dreams, and I'm done talking about them."

My curiosity was at its peak. Was she stuck in that room? Why was she stuck in our house? I needed to see Hannah with my own eyes, no matter how much it would scare me. Tonight . . . tonight was the night.

Luckily, the school day went by easily enough. With the

exception of Matt Kingston's slimy mug, the morning went pretty smoothly. Sally Hirsch was all smiles again because she and Jesse Mills were still an item. Despite her erratic behavior, I couldn't help but feel happy for her. She told me how nice he was, and how he wrote her a poem. Then, to my horror, she took it out and recited it to me. I respectfully listened to her, and begrudgingly told her it was really sweet.

Then there was art class, and Megan was hard at work painting a rendition of Vincent van Gogh's *The Starry Night*. She and I talked about the upcoming weekend—I was having my friends over and she was going to the graveyard to trace tombstones. I guess everyone had their own idea of fun. Spanish went smoothly, and Kristy Meyers was actually quiet. I'd heard she and Matt had been having problems lately. Word had been spreading about Matt being involved in something unseemly. I don't know, they were just rumors; but apparently, he had some dark secret. Poor girl—I actually felt sorry for her. Having to look at his face every day . . . I laughed under my breath and Kristy looked up at me. *Oops.*

Finally, lunchtime came. Amy and Max were at our table already and they both greeted me with a "Hey, Jess!" when I sat down. We talked about how fun tonight would be.

"My mom's ordering pizza for us."

"That's so crazy because I have, like, been craving pizza all week!" Max blurted out.

"Max, you *always* crave pizza," Amy snickered.

What she said wasn't even funny, but for some reason, I laughed so hard at Amy's comment that chocolate milk flew out of my nose. Max drew back, disgusted.

"That's so gross, Jess!"

"I'm *sorry*! I think I'm slaphappy. I'm gonna die of a laugh attack."

"Ha, that's a new one—laugh attack." Max studiously wrote the phrase on an imaginary board with an imaginary pencil.

"So, what else are we gonna do?" Amy asked. "Scary movies?" She rubbed her palms together, sporting an evil face.

"Pfft!" Max dismissed the thought with a wave of her hand. "Like Jess hasn't seen 'em all already."

"Actually, I think I might have something a lot *scarier*."

Amy and Max quickly fell silent.

"What do you mean?" Amy asked, head tilted and eyes squinting with curiosity.

"Yeah, uh, what could be *scarier*?" Max asked, intrigued.

"Well . . . I didn't really want to tell you guys this *now*. But I just can't hold it in any longer!" I blurted out.

"Well, c'mon already! What is it?" Max was clapping her hands with excitement.

"It's actually about that girl."

"What girl? You mean, *Hannah*?" Amy spoke very slowly.

"Yeah."

Max broke the brief silence. "What *about* her?"

"Okay, well . . . I'm not even sure that anything is going to happen. I mean, I don't even know what's up there, if *anything*. There's this room up by the attic. Like, just some weird little room. And ever since we moved in, I just . . . I can't stop thinking about it." I leaned in, speaking softer. "It's like the only part of the house I haven't seen yet, you know? And you guys talked about voodoo stuff happening up there. Sure, nothing happened when my parents checked it out, but that was in the middle of the day. What's it like . . . at night?"

Max and Amy briefly exchanged fearful glances, then looked back at me.

"So what are we gonna do?" Amy asked.

"We're gonna go up there, *that's* what we're gonna do. We're gonna go see what's in that room."

7

Ascending Into Darkness

As the day went on, I grew more and more anxious. I felt as if this was all happening too soon. Hell, a couple of times, I even felt like flaking out. As the bell officially ended the last class of the day and we grabbed our backpacks from our lockers, I could feel the tension in the air as we walked to the bus.

"So . . . about tonight, Jess," Amy spoke softly, the tone someone uses when they're asking for forgiveness.

"Yeah?"

"Well, I don't know. Do you really want to do this? I mean, what if there's something really *bad* in that room?"

"No . . . *Amy!*" I turned toward her, pleading with my arms outstretched. "You can't wuss out! I have to do this . . . *we* have to do this. I *need* you guys. I can't do this on my own."

"C'mon, it won't be that bad," Max chimed in. "I mean, worst case scenario, there's like some dead body up there and we just make a run for it."

Amy wasn't amused. "That's *not* funny, Max!"

"Sorry. Just tryin' to lighten the mood a little, *geez* . . ."

"Yeah, and believe me—if there were a dead body up there,

we'd be *smellin'* it," I said.

"*See!*" Max raised her arms up. Then, looking at me, dropped them. "Eww, that's gross."

"This is blackmail . . ." Amy muttered.

"It's not blackmail! Look, it's not gonna be that bad. We'll have a flashlight and everything—it'll be fine."

"What do you mean, *flashlight?*" Max stopped in her tracks, arms crossed.

"Well." I paused and looked at them sheepishly. "There's no light switch in the hallway, so we'll need a flashlight."

"Oh, *hell* no! Are you crazy? There's no light switch?" Max paused before going on. "Why the hell would there be a hallway where you can't see where you're going?"

"I don't know." I laughed nervously. "I guess that's just how the place was built, with no light switch. Pretty stupid, I know."

"Well that's just *great*," Amy joked sarcastically. "Hey, if I like, freeze in shock or something, you guys better carry me out. Oh, wait . . . you won't be able to *see* me!"

We fell silent as we walked side by side. The subject had become trying, but I knew they were in. I felt it. Hell, they were my best friends—wasn't that what friends were for? I kept my cool on the outside while we rode home, but inside I was a mess. Anything could happen tonight, and I knew they were putting their safety in my hands. Who really knew what was up there? Safety in numbers . . . Taking a deep breath in, I laid my head against the window and watched as the colors whizzed by.

When the bus stopped at Wicker Grove, Amy and Max gasped.

"Yeah, welcome to *my* side of town," I said sarcastically.

"Oh, it's . . . it's *nice*, Jess. I mean, lots of trees and grass and, yeah—nice and green." Amy glanced at me with a forced smile.

"Thanks, Amy, but you don't have to."

"Don't have to what?"

"I know it's hella weird. It ain't like Crescent Lane, that's for sure."

To be quite honest, sometimes I imagined Wicker Grove was an old dirt road. So much in fact that at times I'd pictured myself as a cowgirl out of an old Western—spurs clanging as my boots scuffed the dirt, hands in the pockets of my dusty blue jeans, and a handkerchief around my neck. Oh yeah, and a cute cowgirl hat to top it off. I smiled at the thought.

As we got off the bus and walked to my house, I marveled at their wide-eyed curiosity. They looked like little children experiencing a carnival for the first time. Looking up, left, right, ahead, behind—all the while unaware.

"So, what do you guys think?"

"Um, it's *different* . . . that's for sure. Definitely not anything like Crescent Lane." Amy looked up, spanning the canopy of trees above us. "What is this, like a ceiling? What's with the trees? They're so . . . *branchy*."

Max and I both laughed.

"What? What's so funny?"

"Nothing—just that *branchy* is a funny word."

"Well, what *else* would you call it, Max?"

"True . . . Maybe they're gonna swallow us up *whole*!" Max clawed at the air with her hands, growling.

"You're a weirdo, Max. I like them," I said, smiling.

Amy and Max fell silent.

"Well, there ya go. I like 'em too, Jess. Just a whole lot more Mother Nature than we're used to, that's all. It's a *good* thing." Max cocked her head and smiled.

"It is, right?" I took a deep breath in and enthusiastically announced our arrival. "Two-seven-four Wicker Grove, here we are!"

"So this is two-seven-four Wicker Grove . . ." Amy looked up, forefinger on her chin. "It looks like a nice enough place. I mean, not the kind of place where, you know . . . someone, you know . . ."

"*Died?*" Max finished Amy's sentence. "Was that the word you were fishin' for?"

"Um, yeah. Thanks, Max."

"It's not as bad as you guys think. It's not, like, some horrible place. It's actually quite charming inside. It grows on you, believe me."

As we walked up to the porch, I stared at the little window above both Ben's room and mine—that mysterious black hole we were going to explore tonight. Shivering, I rubbed my arms.

"You all right, Jess?" Amy looked concerned.

"Yeah, I'm all right. Just thinking about later tonight, ya know?"

"Yeah, I know," she sighed.

"Hey, let's try and have a little fun, shall we? Before all hell breaks loose? Maybe literally?" Max joked.

"Yeah. Sounds like a plan." As I opened the front door, the sweet smell of pepperoni pizza filled the air.

"Hey, Mom!"

"Oh, hey! Just in time—pizza just got here."

We all set our backpacks down and headed for the kitchen.

"Hi, Mrs. Kierney!" Amy and Max chimed.

"Hi, girls! How *are* you? I feel like I haven't seen you in ages!"

"I know, it feels like a really long time," Amy said.

"Yeah, well, moving kinda put a damper on that. But now we're all settled in, and the place just couldn't be nicer." My mom smiled ear to ear as she set the table for us. She loved when Amy and Max came over.

"I love this *kitchen*!" Max gasped. "It's absolutely beautiful! And you have an island . . . ooh, always wanted an island." She ran her fingers over the top of it. "Our kitchen's so small, we don't even have space for one."

I smiled. "It's pretty nice. I mean, to have all this space in the kitchen. Never feels crowded, even with us all in here."

"Yeah, I bet," Amy said. "Our kitchen's small too. This house—it's so much bigger than your old house."

"New house, so many rooms—can't wait to look around!" Max rubbed her hands together with a big grin on her face.

"Well, you guys can have all the looking around you want. Just eat this pizza first before it gets cold. Then Jess can give you the grand tour."

"Thanks, Mrs. Kierney," Amy said.

"Yeah, thanks!" Max chimed in.

"You're very welcome, girls. Mind if I join you?"

"Of *course* not." I moved over and she sat next to me. We all enjoyed dinner together, and Max and Amy updated my mom on the latest news about them and their families.

After we'd eaten and cleaned up, I asked my mom where Dad and Ben were.

"Oh, Dad took Ben and Owen to the movies. They'll be back later."

"Oh, cool. Okay, well, I'm gonna show them the backyard."

"Just be careful. There's a big forest back there, and I don't want you guys walking too far off. Lord knows what's in there."

"Sure thing, Mrs. Kierney. We'll keep Jess safe." Max patted my back.

"Pfft, whatever. More like I'll keep *you* safe, Miss I'm Too Curious for My Own Good. How many times have you gotten us lost, Max?"

"Pay her no mind, Mrs. Kierney. Little white lies—don't know where they come from. I'm an expert navigator."

"Yeah, *right*," Amy joked.

"Hey, this is slander!"

"You girls are too much," my mom laughed. "Just go have fun."

I was excited we had most of the evening to ourselves and had no idea Ben was going to the movies tonight with Owen. Poor Ben—Owen was his only friend. They were both pretty quirky, but at least they had each other.

As we stepped outside, Max stopped abruptly. "Man, your backyard is *huge*! I mean, *look* at it! Your yard on Crescent Lane was, like, less than half this size. Holy crap!"

Amy and Max still lived near Crescent Lane. They were within walking distance of each other, and both had yards almost identical to my old one.

"I know, it's crazy. Took me a while to get used to, but now I really like it. Makes me feel a little more free or something."

We walked out onto the deck and breathed in the fresh air.

"Oh, man, I love this." Max closed her eyes, taking in a deep breath.

"I know, doesn't it smell great?"

"Yeah, Jess, it's like you can smell everything—the leaves, the grass . . . so fresh."

"I know."

They followed me down the steps, and we all came to a halt in the middle of the yard.

"Wow, I feel *really* small."

"Yeah, no kidding, Ames. That forest looks like it could swallow us up whole. Forget those crazy branchy trees by the street, this has them trumped." Max laughed. "You ever go in there?" she asked me.

"*Hell* no. There's no way I'm gonna step foot in there. It's too creepy, and it's so thick. I mean, *look* at it. I don't know how it survives—it looks like everything is strangled and suffocated, and yet, it just thrives."

"Yeah, that's weird." Amy scanned the thick brush.

"Your yard's so empty—there's nothing here except for those little pine trees all the way over there. That's funny, they're so out of place." Max pointed over to them.

"Yeah, I know. My mom plans on starting a garden over there soon. It's weird, though. I mean, when I come out here, it feels so nice to have all this space. But at the same time, I always feel a little uncomfortable because there's almost *too* much of it, you know?"

"Yeah, I definitely hear ya on that," Amy agreed.

"Hey, I wanna show you guys something."

"What?" Max asked.

"Here, by the pine trees. C'mon." They followed me over. I wanted to show them the doll I found to see what they thought about it. As we neared the pine trees, they followed me to the back side of the trees.

"I found this d—" I suddenly stopped dead in my tracks.

"You found what?" Amy looked confused.

"Where'd it *go*? It was just . . . I just saw it last weekend." I circled around, eager to spot the doll's little grin. "I found this little porcelain doll here before—right here behind the pine trees. It was just staring up at me. I think it may have been . . ." *Why was Hannah dressed just like this doll in my nightmares? She wore a blue dress in Ben's dreams too.*

"Hannah's?" Amy finished.

"Yeah . . . Hannah's."

"Maybe it was," Max agreed. "It *had* to be. I mean, they were the last ones to live in this house before you guys moved in."

"That's creepy." Amy hugged herself. "Gives me the chills just thinking about it—I'm getting goose bumps."

"But who would *move* it? I mean, if it was here all this time, why'd it disappear right *now*?"

"I dunno, maybe a dog got to it, or maybe some wild animal. Who knows?" Max shrugged.

"Yeah, I guess you're right. It's just . . . weird." I stared at the empty spot behind the pine trees as my mind searched for a rational explanation for why the doll had disappeared.

"C'mon, Jess. Let's go inside. I wanna see your room. And it's gettin' a little chilly out here," Max pleaded.

"Yeah, enough of this Hannah stuff. It's creepin' me out." Amy shuddered.

"Okay, okay. Let's go. But don't forget about later tonight, guys. I'll show you the stairway up to the attic. Can't miss it—it's right between my room and Ben's."

Amy and Max both gulped. "Yeah, Jess. We're still in."

When we got back inside, my mom was talking to her friend on the phone.

"Oh, hold on a sec, Gayle," she said. "Hi, girls. Did you show them upstairs yet, Jess?"

"No, we were just out back lookin' around."

"Okay, well let me know if you need anything."

"Thanks, Mom." I walked my friends to the stairs and we stood there, looking up.

"My room's on the left, Ben's is on the right, and the stairway that leads up to the attic is smack in the middle."

We all glanced up toward the door in the middle as we ascended the steps slowly.

"That's our mission, guys—what's behind that door," Max said sarcastically.

"Max, it's not funny. I'm still scared."

"I am too, Amy. Believe me . . . Do you guys want to see the stairs to the attic?"

"Yeah, I guess. Lay it on us." Max said.

"Okay." I reached out—in slow motion, it seemed—to grab the doorknob. No one made a sound. Slowly, turning the knob, I heard a click. Then, after taking a deep breath, I opened the door. It opened easily and, as always, I felt a cool draft of air brush my face.

"Why is it so *cold*? And where's that draft coming from?" Amy asked.

"Your guess is as good as mine. It's always like that every time anyone opens this door. It goes away, but it's always there."

Finally, the door was wide open. All three of us stood still, staring up the stairway. At the very top, the steps continued into blackness.

"Where does it end?"

"I don't know, Ames. I guess we'll find out. It can't be *that* long, right? I mean, there can't be that many steps."

"You don't even know what's *up* there, Jess. I mean, what if there's like cobwebs and spiders and stuff? There's *no* way I'm walking through that!" Amy defiantly crossed her arms.

"Amy, spiders are the *least* of my fears."

"Hey, you!"

We all screamed, terrified and clinging onto each other for dear life. Ben stood at the bottom of the stairs, laughing hysterically.

"Haha, I got you!"

"Ben, that's not funny!" I screamed.

"Better not go up there, I'll tell Mom and Dad."

"You're a brat." I slammed the door shut.

Maybe I really should listen to Mom and Dad on this one, though.

That night, we all decided the only way to get into the right mindset was to tell each other ghost stories. Max said it would be the best way to prepare for our ghost hunt, but I really thought she was just trying to scare the crap out of us for her own guilty pleasure.

"Max, *c'mon*! Your stories are totally creepin' me out. I mean, severed heads floating down stairways and poltergeists slamming doors and dragging people out of their beds. Not cool! If anything, you're just scarin' the crap out of Jess and me."

"Amy, you *know* they're not real. They're just a bunch of urban legends."

Amy huffed and crossed her arms.

"Guys, fighting is not gonna help the situation. We're a team, remember?" I took a deep breath and let it out slowly. "Let's do this."

"Wait . . . are you really ready?" Max asked sincerely.

"Scaredy cat," Amy mocked.

"*Amy!*" Max took my pillow and whopped her in the face.

"Good one, Ames." We high-fived each other.

"You guys are ridiculous, you know that?" Max got to her feet. "C'mon, let's go."

"Wait . . ." I scrambled for the flashlight. "Okay, now we're ready."

"Do we need anything else?"

"Yeah, Max, maybe some sanity?" Amy joked.

"I think we could *all* use some of that right now. Honestly, though, I think we're good with just the flashlight. I wish we could leave the hallway light on, but I don't want to wake up

Ben or my parents."

"Oh, great." Amy sighed. "No lights at all? Just the flashlight?"

"I'm afraid so—this guy's our one-way . . . err . . . two-way ticket there and back." I tapped the flashlight against my doorframe as we stepped into the hallway.

"Who's gonna open the door?" asked Amy.

"I'll open it," Max said.

"No, I got it—my house, my door. I'll do the honors."

Max and Amy stepped aside as I slowly turned the doorknob. Just as expected, a frigid breeze swept over us.

"God, I hate that," I said as I took my first step into the hallway. I turned around to make sure Max and Amy were right behind me. "Wingmen?"

"Wing*women*. But yes," Max said.

"Okay, good."

There was no railing, so footing was my only guide. Slowly, I placed my right foot on the first step and gulped nervously. Second step, third step—I stopped to look behind me. Max and Amy were there, wide-eyed and alert as hell. I could hear all of us breathing, Amy a little quicker than Max and me.

"We're right here, Jess," Max whispered.

I smiled and cautiously turned my attention back to the stairway. Fourth step, fifth, sixth, seventh, eighth . . . at the eleventh step, I paused. *"Jesus,"* I whispered. "How many freakin' steps are there?"

"I don't like this," Amy whimpered.

"I'm sorry, Amy. But please, hold it together—we're almost there."

"How do you *know*?!"

I didn't, and that's what scared the hell out of me. "I just do," I lied.

After the fifteenth step, I began to shake. Claustrophobia was kickin' in. The hallway was narrow and we were already up so high. Just thinking that all of us were fifteen steps from the safety of the hub of our house scared me. It was like we were in an upward wormhole, aimlessly moving forward blindly. I placed my foot on the next step. Sixteen, seventeen, eighteen . . . then on the twentieth step, my foot hit level flooring. I gasped, shocked and relieved at the same time. Here we all were—twenty steps away from safety and in alien territory. Just us three girls with something to prove.

Max and Amy stepped up to where I was, and I felt one of them seek my hand and grasp it. "Who's this?"

"It's me," Amy answered. "I'm scared."

"It's okay, Amy. We're all together. Don't worry."

"Yeah," Max said. "Don't sweat it, Ames. We're fine."

I shone my flashlight straight ahead. "Oh, my God!" Gasping, I dropped the flashlight on the floor. It fell and hit the ground with a heavy thud. Max and Amy jumped, and I could hear their feet scatter about nervously.

"It's there, right in front of us—the room!" I gulped, picked up the flashlight, and with shaking hands, pointed the light straight ahead. There was the door in front of us, leading to the room that had haunted me ever since we'd moved here. I was finally facing my fears.

"Well, what do we do now?" Amy asked.

"We open it." I could feel the tension among us as I reached for the doorknob. It was cold, and the thought of what my hand was clasping made me shiver. "Okay, here goes nothing," I said as I turned the knob. I heard it click and, shutting my eyes, slowly opened the door. It creaked incessantly.

When I felt the doorknob hit the wall, I opened my eyes, shone the flashlight straight ahead, and gasped. This was not a storage room—it was a real room. There was a bed up against the wall on the left. It was very small, and it had a beautiful, plush red comforter. In the middle of the room, there was a red oval shag rug, the same deep red color as the bedding. The walls and the floor were all wood, and I could smell the earthy cedar. The walls were bare; there were no pictures or decorations of any sort. And on the wall to the right, there was a little white desk with a half-burnt candle placed in the center. A white chair with red roses painted along the top was in front of the desk. I heard Max and Amy gasp behind me.

There was a small circular window at the far end of the room facing the street, through which the moonlight was softly filtering through. It was almost . . . magical. And peaceful.

"Jess, what *is* this? Why the hell is there a bedroom all the way up here?" Amy asked.

"I don't know . . ."

"M-maybe this is a guest room?" Amy stuttered. The uncertainty in her voice confirmed that not even she believed what she was saying.

"I don't think so," Max answered slowly.

The peacefulness I felt in this room filled me with complete tranquility. It was so small and quiet, so cozy, so . . . isolated from the rest of the house. I pointed the flashlight back toward the bed, and what I saw made me freeze. There, resting on the pillow, was the porcelain doll I'd seen in the backyard.

"Oh my God . . ." I whispered.

"Jess, what is it?"

"Holy shit!" I said, placing my hand over my mouth in complete shock. There it was—the doll I'd discovered when we'd first moved here . . . the same exact doll. And it had just

. . . appeared. I could've sworn it wasn't there when we first opened the door.

"You guys, that doll," I pointed at the bed. "That's the doll I was going to show you out back—that's the doll I found by the pine trees."

"Oh, my God." Amy leaped back and covered her mouth. "Jess, that doll wasn't here when we first came in here."

"I know!" I whispered loudly back.

Max just stood there, trying to process what was going on. "What the hell? Maybe it was there and we just didn't see it. C'mon, guys, dolls don't just mysteriously materialize out of nothingness. It *must* have been there before—"

Suddenly, the candle on top of the desk lit up. We all stared in complete horror as the flame ignited itself.

"Holy *shit*," Max said under her breath. And without even thinking, I ran out of the room behind Amy and Max, who had started running out a second before me. I stumbled down the stairs, losing my footing a couple of times and dropping the flashlight. It knocked on each step, throwing eerie streaks of light everywhere.

"You guys, *wait!*" As soon as I got out, I slammed the door behind me, panting uncontrollably. How that sound didn't wake up Ben or my parents was beyond me, but thank God it didn't.

We couldn't sleep that night. In fact, for the first few minutes, we hardly even talked. What had just happened did not seem real. It felt like we'd all been dreaming and were waiting to wake up. And then there was that overwhelming feeling of dread. My house was haunted . . . I obviously lived in a haunted house because what happened up there was unexplainable.

"Jess?" Amy broke the silence. "Are you okay?"

I was looking down at my fingers, in awe of how long and slender they were, a completely random thought at a time like this. "Yeah . . . I'm okay," I whispered.

"What about you, Max? You okay?"

"Yeah, I'm okay. Just, well, pretty freaked out." She laughed nervously.

"I think that goes for all of us," I said. "I mean, seriously, what the hell just *happened*? That doll—that *freaky* doll—I can't get it out of my head." I cradled my head on my knees and rocked myself back and forth. Then the tears came, and they came hard. Sobbing, I buried my face in my hands. Amy and Max glanced at each other and then embraced me. We all just sat there, holding one another for what seemed like forever. This was real, and now we were all in it together.

8

Ghostly Signs

The next day at breakfast, my mom asked us about the previous night. "I heard this loud bang, like a door slamming. What on earth were you guys doing?"

They heard it. I opened my mouth to tell her a big fat lie, but Max came to the rescue.

"Oh, we were just playing hide-and-seek, Mrs. Kierney. We got a little carried away." She shot me a wink and playfully elbowed me.

"Hide-and-seek? You guys still *play* that?"

"Yeah," I said sheepishly, giving Max a *what the hell was that* look. "I guess we still get a little carried away."

"Yeah, I'd say *so*." My mom chuckled. "I'm surprised you didn't wake your little brother."

"Oh, he'll sleep through *anything*." I glanced over at the den where Ben was playing video games.

"Well, next time just try to keep it a little more quiet."

"We will, Mrs. Kierney. Sorry," innocent doe-eyed Amy chimed in.

"Thanks, Amy. Well, you girls finish your breakfast. What

time are your parents picking you up?"

Max looked at the clock. "Oh, my mom's picking Amy and me up at twelve."

"Okay, good. Jess, do you want to go to the nursery with me after they leave? I was planning on going around twelve anyway, so we can make it a lunch date."

"Sure, Mom."

"Great." She patted my shoulder as she left the kitchen.

We finished breakfast and then walked out on the deck. Amy and Max sat down on the deck chairs and I leaned my back against the railing, eyes closed and bathing in the sun's luxurious morning rays.

"So, what are we gonna do *now*?" Amy asked.

"What do you *mean*, what are we gonna do?" Max replied.

"Well, aren't we gonna *tell* someone?"

"No," I snapped. Amy coiled back. "Sorry Ames, I just . . . I don't think we should tell anyone."

"Why *not*? I mean, shouldn't we at least tell your *parents*? It's their house too."

"No, I can't. I don't want them to know. Besides, I don't think they'd believe me."

"Of *course* they'd believe you. Why *wouldn't* they?"

"They just wouldn't. Adults don't believe in stuff like this. Probably why nothing happened when they walked in that room," Max answered.

"Yep. I think we should just keep this thing between us, okay?"

"Yeah, that's best," Max agreed.

"I guess . . . but I still don't understand why we can't tell anyone," Amy said. Our eyes met, and she read the exhaustion on my face. "Okay, Jess. I promise I won't tell."

For the rest of the morning, we decided to enjoy ourselves

and put the uneasiness we all felt behind us for at least a little while. I grabbed my basketball, and we played a few games of H-O-R-S-E. As we hugged each other before they parted, I felt a deeper connection because of the secret we now shared.

After they left, my mom and I went to the nursery. Her friend Gayle had given her advice on what vegetables to buy for her garden, and she couldn't wait to start gathering the seeds for her collection. I was aching to tell her about last night, and part of me felt that by not telling her, I was lying. It hurt, but I didn't break down. It was so hard to keep this to myself, but I figured that eventually there would be a time and a place for it. Putting my worries at bay, I delighted in touching the soft flower petals and walking among the colors of spring. Afterward, we grabbed some lunch.

"So, did you guys have fun last night? How'd Amy and Max like the house?"

"They really like it, especially the backyard. Once I took them out there, it was funny—they were, like, blown away at the amount of space."

"I can imagine. Our old backyard was really small. And to think that back then we thought it was big!"

"Yeah, pretty funny." I laughed. "It was so nice to have them over. We had a good time. Just nice to hang out again . . ."

"Hide-and-seek?" my mom quipped.

I felt horrible having to lie through my teeth. "Well, you know . . . it was *fun*! Besides, when was the last time *you* played hide-and-seek?"

"Oh, I don't know." She ran her fingers through her bangs. "I guess those days are long gone for me, huh? We used to play when you and your brother were little, but these days—I'm just Mom." While saying this, she laid both palms firmly on the table.

"Aww, Mom. You're not *just* a mom. You're so much more too."

She smiled and cupped her hand lovingly over mine. "Thanks, Jess. You can be a mystery to me sometimes, but I love you."

You can be a mystery sometimes . . . yeah, mystery is right. If only you knew.

"I love you too."

That night after dinner, I went out on the deck to get some quiet time and organize my thoughts. This was my new favorite place. The air was warm, and a soft breeze caressed my skin. I sat down, closed my eyes, and thought of feathers floating through the air and brushing my face. Peaceful, tranquil . . . and then an image of the room popped into my head. Startled, my eyes shot open. The forest lay straight ahead, a dark abyss with no end in sight. And I felt sad—maybe that was where Hannah was. She lived in blackness, in some never-ending void, and she couldn't find her way out. Tirelessly trudging through the blackness, branches whipping her face and cutting her ankles. Looking for help, screaming, crying in the darkness. But there was no one. At least not yet . . .

"What you doing, Jess?"

I gasped and turned around, hands on my chest. "*Jesus*, Ben. You scared me."

"Sorry. Didn't mean to give you a *heart attack*." He sat down next to me. "What'd you guys do last night? I heard stuff."

"Oh, we were just playing hide-and-seek, that's all."

"That's weird," he said.

I laughed. "Yeah, I know . . . it *is* weird."

"Well, I'm younger than you and even *I* don't do that." He

pointed at himself in high regard.

"Thanks," I smirked. "Hey, did you ever go upstairs? To the attic?"

"No, why?"

"Oh, just wondering." I clasped my hands together and leaned on my elbows, dreamily staring off into the woods.

Ben looked puzzled. "I don't really think there's much up there."

"Yeah, I guess it's not really a big deal," I said, staring off. Is it weird that he doesn't like exploring? Doesn't every kid like exploring? Especially boys? Then I turned around and looked directly at him. "Hey, have you talked to . . . that little girl in your dream? I mean, lately?"

"No." He looked down at his hands.

"What do you think happened to her?"

"I don't know, but I don't think it was good."

"Yeah, me neither. She never said anything about it in your dreams?"

"No, she never said anything."

I had considered telling Ben about how the girl in his dreams had been a real, living person named Hannah, but had decided against it. Knowing that a child had just disappeared one day from the house we were now living in would be terrifying for him. I wished *I* didn't know.

Wanting to change the topic altogether, I said, "Hey, you want some ice cream?" The unknown was eating at me and making me anxious.

"Yeah!"

"Okay, cool. C'mon—I'll make you a famous Jess Kierney sundae."

School dragged on that week. Every day seemed like it lasted longer and longer, and I just couldn't wait for the weekend. Amy and Max felt the same way. At lunch, we talked about school gossip—who was dating who, and who was mad at who. I think in the back of our minds, though, we were all thinking about the room. Although we didn't bring it up too often, it was still there, lingering. They seemed to be pushing it to the side, just trying to forget. It seemed like they wanted to move on; they were done.

"So, what do you guys think we should do next? I mean, we just can't stop investigating. We have to go further."

"What *can* we do? I mean, honestly—I think we should just forget about it, you know?" Max said.

"I don't know. I mean, part of me feels that the doll appeared there for a reason. I feel like, like . . . it was a sign. A sign that we have to do something."

"Do *what?*"

"I don't know yet."

Max looked at Amy and rolled her eyes slightly.

I sighed, frustrated. "What about you, Amy? What do *you* think? I mean, don't you think we should *do* something? It just feels right." Amy scratched her head and leaned her elbow on the table, glancing at Max.

"I don't know, Jess. I mean, I think Max is right. The only thing you *could* do is hire someone who specializes in the supernatural. You know, to investigate it properly."

"And how the hell am I supposed to do *that* with my parents around and only a couple hundred bucks to my name?"

"*Exactly.*"

"I just don't know. That's the worst part about it." I looked at them for some reaction and maybe some support, but I got nothing. Just then, the bell rang and lunch was over.

"Sorry, Jess. See you in English," Max said as she and Amy left. I just sat there for a second, thinking about what had happened Friday night, and how we had all felt a deeper connection—at least *I* had. Maybe I was overanalyzing, reading too much into this. But then there was the other part, and this part was *strong*. This part said it was my responsibility to discover the truth about that room. And in doing so, discover the truth about what happened to Hannah. Why were Max and Amy avoiding it? I *needed* them.

Later that afternoon, Mrs. Rosen was all smiles when I walked into English class, and it made me forget about lunch.

"Hi, Mrs. Rosen."

"Hi, Jess. How's your day going?"

"Oh, I'm good. Just excited about the weekend." I did my best to sound genuine. I really just wanted to find out more about that room, but wasn't about to tell her about everything.

"Yes, me too. Do you have any plans?"

"Oh, no. I think I'm just gonna catch up on some reading, maybe watch some movies. No biggies."

"Well, that sounds nice."

"Mrs. Rosen?"

"Yes?"

I paused before going on because I knew it was gonna sound weird.

"Do you believe in ghosts?"

"Oh . . ." She seemed taken aback. "Well, I *guess* so. I do believe that something happens after death. I don't know if that's the right answer, but it's what I believe. And in *that* way, I guess I do believe in ghosts." She looked puzzled. "Why do you ask?"

"Well, to be honest, reading *The Crucible* kind of got me

thinking about it. Just the whole witchcraft thing—supernatural events, ghosts, all that."

"Oh, well, I don't mean for this book to *scare* you—" she began.

"Oh no, I'm not scared," I interrupted. *Liar, Jess!* "Sorry, I didn't mean to interrupt."

"Oh, no, go on . . ."

"I'm not scared, I just . . . I guess it's mostly curiosity about signs and stuff like that."

"Signs?" She was leaning back on her desk, facing me with arms folded. I had her complete attention. *I love how Mrs. Rosen listens to me.*

"Yeah. Just weird things that happen, you know? Sometimes I think things happen for a reason. And sometimes I think things call out to you . . ." I trailed off.

"Jess, is everything all right?"

"Oh, yeah," a little embarrassed. "I'm fine."

She glanced at the clock. It was about five minutes until class started and the other students would be arriving soon.

"Well, Jess, all I can say is . . . if you're *seeing* something, or if you've had a sign of some kind . . . don't do anything you don't feel right about or that doesn't feel safe. Just trust your judgment, you're a smart girl."

She smiled at me, then turned and started organizing papers for class. Mrs. Rosen had given me hope—hope that what I was about to do was okay.

9

Introducing Megan Pierce

On Friday, all I could think about was Megan. Though Megan and I were not close friends by any means, I believed she was the only person who could help me right now. Maybe it was a long shot, but I had to talk to her about this. As I walked into art class that morning, I saw Megan as I had never seen her before. There she sat, dressed head to toe in black, gently smoothing the creases of a clay sculpture she'd begun last week. Her fingers glided over the sculpture effortlessly, as if they were works of art themselves. She looked beautiful, actually, lost in her craft. And this morning, unlike any other morning, her dark energy seemed inviting.

"Hey, Megan." I sat down next to her.

"Hey, Jess . . ." she answered, a little accusatory.

"Oh, I'm sorry. I didn't mean to interrupt you. Your sculpture is beautiful, though, really."

At that, she stopped and stared at me, her hands hovering over the sculpture. *"Really?"*

"Yes, I really like it. I think it's . . . kind of haunting. In a *good* way, if that makes sense."

We both looked at it. It was a demon. He was kneeling and his arms were reaching up with hands like claws. His wings wrapped around him, as if to envelope him from harm.

"Thanks, Jess. That means a lot. I've been working so hard on this. It kinda feels like part of me now, ya know?"

"Yeah, I get what you mean," I said, even though the thought kind of irked me. "Uh, Megan? I got a question."

"Shoot."

"Well, I feel kind of silly asking, but I thought you might be able to help me."

"I'm listening," she said as her fingers smoothed the arched wings.

"Do you know anything about . . . ghosts?"

She stopped abruptly and swiveled her chair so that she was facing me front and center.

"Ghosts? Yeah, of course. I read books about that stuff all the time. The supernatural, life after death—I believe in all that stuff." She then sighed. "I've never seen a ghost *myself*, but I know some people who have. So I totally believe in them. Why do you ask?"

I told her everything that had been happening, up until the night Amy, Max, and I had found the room. Megan listened intently the whole time. I knew she would, and it felt good to have her undivided attention.

"*Whoa*," she said when I had finished.

"What?"

"Well, it just seems like there's unfinished business there."

"What do you *mean*, unfinished business?"

"Well, it doesn't seem like things are settled there." A chill ran up my spine and I had this crazy vision of a poltergeist making our lives hell because things were not *settled*.

"Look, you wouldn't be feeling any of the emotions you are or seeing any of the things you're seeing if everything was *fine*. There's something that needs to be . . . discovered."

I was leaning toward her, legs crossed and my chin buried in my palm. "But *what?*" I pleaded. This was the question that had been consuming my thoughts day after day, night after night. This was the question that Max and Amy did not want to help me find an answer to. Megan picked up her pencil and flip-flopped it between her fingers. I sat still, anticipating her answer. And as she opened her mouth, my eyes widened.

"I . . . I don't know."

And at that, I sank down into my seat again.

"No." She lay her hand down on my desk. "Don't get *discouraged*. I mean, I think I might know what you have to do."

My eyes widened again as the anticipation killed me. "What do I have to do?"

"You have to talk to Hannah."

I felt the color drain from my face.

"Jess, are you all right?"

"Y-yeah, I'm fine. It's just . . . you're telling me I have to talk to a *dead* girl."

"Don't think of it that way. She's a ghost. She's already gone physically, but her spirit's still there, and *that's* the problem. My mom always says that happy spirits move on. But spirits in turmoil—they don't go anywhere. They're restless, and they can't move on until the situation imprisoning them is resolved. Hannah's got unfinished business, Jess. That's why she's still there—she's not happy. That's why she's giving you signs. The dreams, the doll, your brother . . . I feel like she talked to your brother to try to get to you somehow. She doesn't want *him* to help her, or else she would have asked him. For some reason, she's chosen you."

Tears blurred my vision.

"Oh, Jess, I'm sorry. Why are you crying?"

"I just, I just feel so bad . . . for Hannah. And I'm scared too."

She placed her hand softly on my shoulder. She was so understanding. Why did I never notice this about her before? "Don't be scared, Jess. Think of this as an adventure. You're on a scavenger hunt, and who knows what you'll unearth? No pun intended." We both kinda chuckled.

"Thanks, Megan. I knew I could talk to you about this."

"No prob, Jess. But promise you'll let me know what happens?"

"I promise."

"And if you need any help, I'm an expert on this stuff. Just ask, and I'm all yours."

"Okay, thanks, I really appreciate it. *Really.*"

"You bet."

I tried my best to put our conversation in art class behind me as I headed to English class later that day. I could tell by talking to Amy and Max earlier in the week that they weren't in with this anymore. Maybe they were scared, or maybe they thought I was a fool for wanting to go further. Either way, I'd forgiven them and had decided to put what happened behind me. Our friendship was worth more than this. In English that day, we discussed our required readings more, and Mrs. Rosen said we would have a quiz on Monday. After class ended, Amy, Max, and I got up and grabbed our books.

"So, any plans this weekend?" Amy asked us.

"I'm going to my uncle's wedding in Larmont," Max said. "The wedding's on Saturday, and we're staying the night. So, unfortunately, we'll be there all weekend." She shrugged.

"Bummer," I said.

"Yeah, I know. Believe me—I don't want to go, but I *have* to."

"What about you, Amy?" I asked.

"Oh, we're having a party for my brother's birthday on Saturday. You can come if you want, Jess. It's friends and family."

"Thanks, Amy. I think I'll have to pass, though. We have plans too."

"So I guess we're all going it alone this weekend, huh?"

"Yeah," Max said. "I'll give you guys a call on Sunday after we get back and stuff."

"Cool," I said, a little bummed.

"Yeah, let's all talk this weekend," Amy said. They started to walk out.

"Hey! You guys want to go get ice cream? I know it's Friday, but . . ."

"Sorry, Jess, can't. I gotta get home."

"Yeah, sorry," Max said. "I gotta get goin' too. Gotta try on my stupid dress one more time."

"You guys suck."

"Oh, *thanks!*" Amy frowned, a hand on her hip.

"I kid, I kid . . ."

"C'mon, Ames. Let's leave Miss Grumpy Pants alone." Max grabbed Amy's arm.

"Love ya." They waved as they headed out the door.

"Yeah, love you too."

That night, after everyone else had gone to bed, I stayed up, restless. Lying on my back and staring at the ceiling, I thought about what Megan had told me. *Unfinished . . . things aren't settled . . . talk to Hannah . . .*

"So what are you gonna do, Jess?" It sounded foolish, talking to myself out loud, and I smirked. What *could* I do? I had to see the room again. But this time, I had to go by myself—no Amy and Max, just me. If Megan was right, then Hannah wanted me to go to her, and me alone. So that's what I had to do, though it scared the crap out of me. Since we moved here, I'd felt its grasp strengthen more each day—the need to visit that room alone. I closed my eyes, took a deep breath, and drifted into dreamland.

There she was again. Hannah stood by my bed, staring down at me. The soft light from the moon caressed her angelic face. She opened her mouth, and as she did, she raised her arm and pointed to my bedroom door. She was just about to talk. *Please tell me something . . . anything.* But a cloud of blackness engulfed her, snarling her fragile frame in its grip. And then she was gone, ripped from my sight again just like that. I was terrified.

"Jess! Jess, it's almost twelve. Are you all right?" My mom was calling to me from the doorway.

"Uh . . . what? Twelve?" I yawned and sat up. "Mom, it's *Saturday.*"

"I know. Just checking in—you're usually awake by now."

"I was really tired last night. And I didn't get a lot of sleep."

"Are you having those nightmares again?"

"Yeah . . . and even before that, I just couldn't get to sleep." I sighed and lay back down, staring at the ceiling again.

"Well, there's some pancakes downstairs if you want some."

I closed my eyes and smiled. "Okay, thanks. I will never get sick of pancakes."

"Well, I should *hope* not. What would your dad *do?*"

"Yeah, good point. He is the pancake master."

"Well, get your little butt downstairs!"

My mom and I spent most of the day together, preparing her garden. She'd decided on her vegetables and was absolutely delighted I wanted to help out.

"I don't have any other plans for today anyway," I'd told her.

"Oh, you aren't getting together with your friends this weekend?" She began digging holes in the dirt.

"No. Max is going to a wedding and Amy's brother is having a birthday party."

"Did she invite you? You've met Amy's brother before, haven't you?"

"Yeah, Amy invited me. I don't want to go, though. I just kind of want to chill out this weekend."

"Well, lucky for me, I have a helper."

"Yes, indeed—little helper at your service." I saluted her.

"So, what are your plans for the rest of the day?"

"Mmm, I don't know . . . Honestly, I haven't really thought about it. Guess I'll probably just catch up on some reading or something."

Taking a break, I lay down on my back, hands behind my head, and stared into brilliant blue skies. It was a perfect sixty degrees, and the sun was glorious. Eyes closed, I blocked everything out and focused only on the soft touch of the spring breeze. It caressed my hands and face and playfully tossed my hair. For once, my mind was blank, and it felt good.

As the day wore on, I caught up on some reading. Mrs. Rosen had asked us to read the next act of *The Crucible*, and to write down questions we had about the play. After talking to Megan on Friday, I realized how little I knew about the situation I was facing. Up until now, I hadn't realized the reality of it— the fact I was preparing to communicate with the paranormal realm. I would be the one initiating the conversation—going into her territory. I'd borrowed books from the library and almost everything I read concurred with what Megan had told me. There was a spirit trying to communicate with me, and the only way she could was if I mentally invited her in. The atmosphere needed to be right. Megan had told me Hannah probably lit the candle last time because she didn't want to attempt communication with my friends there. She wanted me, and me alone.

All of the books I read mentioned the term *purgatory*. I knew what it meant, but for some reason, it was just hard to imagine this situation existing for real. I mean, sure, I'd read about this in ghost stories—but I'd never given it any thought until now. This was where Hannah had to be—purgatory. All signs pointed to this. How horrible for her to be stuck in time and unable to move on until reconciling with someone, or *something*.

The crazy thing was that each spirit's plight was different because not all spirits entered the realm from the same circumstances. Some spirits had committed awful crimes in their lives—even murder—and they were sent to purgatory to suffer until they fully realized the gravity of their sins. And even then, after coming to terms with the unspeakable acts they had committed, some of them were still confined to their interspatial prison forever. Then there were those who had just passed on too early. They weren't ready to leave their lives, and could not accept that theirs had been cut short. In the same way, they had to come to grips with their lot and accept it. Until that realization, they had to wander this destitute realm between space and time. And of course, there were also the poor souls who didn't quite understand why they'd passed on. It wasn't a matter of what they had done when they were living or that they had left this world too early, but rather, it was the nature of their passing that they couldn't come to terms with.

I believed either of the last two had been Hannah's plight. It *had* to be—every time I saw her in a dream or nightmare, she looked sad and confused. I didn't see hatred in her; I just saw a lost soul.

Hannah had been ten years old when she died, at least that's what Amy and Max had told me. To die so young . . . it just wasn't fair. Life could be so cruel. Either Hannah was in turmoil because she had died too young, or she was upset at the nature with which she met her fate. I didn't know which one it was. I thought about the dreams I'd had. In many of them, Hannah was happy until the woman called to her. She'd be dancing in circles, laughing, full of life. Then everything would turn black when this woman called her name. Who was this woman and what had she done to Hannah? Maybe she was her babysitter, or maybe she was an aunt or some other relative. Or maybe she was Hannah's mom? I shivered at the thought. Of *course,* she wasn't. Moms are loving and only wish the best for their children.

I collected my thoughts and gazed out my front window. So many possibilities clouded my mind—too many to be able to grasp just one and run with it. I'd read enough and felt prepared for my deliberate encounter with the paranormal tonight. And surprisingly, the thought did not frighten me anymore. Hannah didn't want to scare me. If she had, I would have known for sure, and would probably be seeing a psychiatrist right now! She needed my help, and I was more than happy to oblige. *I'm here, Hannah. Don't worry. I'm here to help.*

We had an early dinner that night, and afterward, my dad and Ben went to the movies again. They asked me if I wanted to go, but the last thing I wanted to do was sit through a movie with them—much less the action movie they were going to see. Plus, I already had plans for the rest of the night, although these would go into effect after the twilight hour. While my mom watched the news, I sat on the couch on the other side of the room and jotted down some notes to help me get through the night. "Don't get scared" was the first one. Easier written than done, but nonetheless important. The second one was, "Don't be afraid to talk." This was, of course, if Hannah spoke to me. I didn't think I could muster up the courage to talk to her first. Besides, I might scare her off. The third was, "Flashlight!!!" I had put three exclamation marks after this one because it was vitally important. I didn't want to start this thing and then realize I wasn't fully prepared. And the fourth was, "Try to be quiet." I knew this one would be the hardest to follow because if I ended up face-to-face with a ghost, who knows how loud I would scream? Even though the room was isolated from the rest of the house, I didn't want to risk waking anyone up. And I didn't want to be found out. We'd gotten off with Max's pathetic hide-and-seek explanation last time; but this time, it was just me. I wanted to keep this thing under wraps for as long as I could. If my parents or Ben woke up and saw me running out of the stairwell, the questions would never end.

Just then, I glanced at the clock. It was already ten o'clock. Where did the time go? My dad and Ben would be home soon, and off to bed shortly after that. Then the house would be mine.

My mom yawned. "I'm gonna go to bed. Wanted to wait up for Dad and Ben, but I'm just too tired."

"Okay. I'll wait up for them."

"Thanks, hun." She kissed my forehead and walked upstairs.

About a half hour later, my dad and Ben came home and Ben way-too-enthusiastically told me about the movie. I tried my best to listen, but for the most part, all I could catch amid his kicks and driving moves was the fact that there were a lot of car chases and crazy stunts. Pretty much sums up most action movies, I guessed. Then after about fifteen minutes of Ben pretending to be an action hero, my dad finally told him it was getting late and he should go to bed.

"Aww, but Dad!"

"You can show us more of your slick moves tomorrow. Maybe you could teach me some of them." My dad shot me a grin.

"You promise? 'Cause I'm warning ya, I might wear you out. I got a lot of moves!"

"Pinky swear," my dad said, and they locked pinkies.

Then Dad turned to me. "You staying up?"

"Yeah. Just a little longer."

"Okay, don't forget to shut everything off before you head up."

"I won't. Good night!"

"G'night. See you tomorrow, hun."

I waited for them to go to bed, and when it was finally quiet, collected my thoughts in the surrounding silence. Aside from the occasional creaks and groans that came with an old house, there was not a sound. After turning off all the lights downstairs, I headed up to my room, where I lay on my bed to wait for a while. A quick glance at the clock—it was almost midnight. The witching hour. *Here we go, Jess.* Taking in a deep breath, I sat up, grabbed the flashlight, and headed toward my bedroom door. Catching my reflection in the mirror, I stopped abruptly. There I was, Jess the ghost hunter. My gray eyes stared back at me, alert as ever. A couple strands of blonde hair had come loose and hung down the sides of my face, while the rest was bunched up in a messy ponytail. My porcelain skin was white as ever tonight, but I wasn't scared. I could do this. I wasn't gonna back down. "C'mon, Jess. Let's go."

10

A Plea for Help

Creeping lightly toward my bedroom door, I opened it very slowly. The hallway was completely black except for the moonlight faintly pouring in through my window behind me. I turned to the left, facing the door to the stairwell. Not wanting to turn the flashlight on just yet since I was in the hallway, I could make out the shape of the doorknob. There was steely coldness as I grabbed onto it. Then, ever so gently, I opened the door. Slowly, slowly . . . and there was that frigid rush of cold air again. Closing my eyes, I welcomed it this time. Then, taking my first step, I closed the door behind me to conceal my tracks. Never mind what I'd felt before, I was still scared to death. Now that I was in the moment, there was no turning back. It was part of me, and I'd accepted that. I soaked up the comfort of my current location, still in the realm of safety, then continued my ascent.

The stairs in front of me were flooded with light from the flashlight, but I still couldn't see the top of the stairwell. The beam of light waned, and I could barely make out the last step. Closing my eyes for a second, I moved on. The stairwell felt narrower than the last time I'd been here. Claustrophobia overwhelmed me again, and my perspiration increased as anxiety kicked in. Fifteen, sixteen, seventeen . . . I counted the steps as I continued. Finally, I hit the last step, and then I froze. For a split second, I thought about going back downstairs and just forgetting the whole thing—putting everything behind me and continuing life as it had been before Hannah consumed my every waking moment. Yeah, that'd be easy. And easy was good, right? I could just go back to my bedroom, sleep the night away, and wake up tomorrow refreshed and prepared to start anew. But then I thought about Hannah, the precious little girl whose life was cut short. I couldn't back down, it felt selfish. *Stupid, stupid thought.* With my feet placed firmly on the landing, I turned to face the door. It was closed. When Amy, Max, and I had come up here I'd left it open in my haste to escape, or so I remembered. *Hannah, what are you trying to do to me?* Who knew what was waiting for me on the other side of this door? The anticipation I felt wasn't the welcoming kind.

I stalled for a second or two, then reached for the doorknob. Turning it gently, I began pushing the door open. Then, to my utter horror, it opened by itself the rest of the way as if being pulled by an imaginary string. Fixated, I watched as it slowly creaked open, revealing the small room inside that was softly bathed in moonlight.

The candle on the desk was already lit. It cast eerie, flickering shadows across the room, giving the small dwelling a life of its own. As I scanned the room, my gaze stopped abruptly on the bed. There was the doll. Her head lay on the pillow, her arms and legs perfectly placed by her sides. I could feel my heart beat in my chest, thump after thump coursing through me and it felt as if my heart was a hammer.

"Calm down, Jess. It's okay." The weird thing was that the silence and the strewn shadows were suddenly comforting; and to my surprise, I felt a sense of calm. Taking in a deep breath and holding it in, I slowly exhaled, closing my eyes as the breath left me and welcomed this moment. *You have to invite her in.* The warm scent of cedar again was invigorating. And that bed—it was so adorable, covered with the plushest bedding I had ever laid my eyes on, and in the most beautiful shade of ruby. It seemed to beckon me. Mesmerized, I stepped inside, and the muffled sound of my footsteps reverberated off the walls.

I reached out my hand and touched the bedspread with my fingertips, gliding them slowly over the soft fabric. The bed was real—everything in here I could touch with my own hands. It was almost as if I needed to touch it for confirmation and validation that I wasn't dreaming. I stopped short of the doll, and gave the bedspread one final caress. Staring at the wall in front of me, I reached out to touch its smooth surface. The walls were so beautiful, and the cedar appeared to writhe in the candlelight as if it were alive.

Then I turned and looked at the little desk, where the candle continued to flicker softly. I reached out to touch the surface. It felt grainy, and as my eyes began to focus on the flickering shadow, I could see scratches on the surface. I couldn't make out whether they formed words or not, so I bent down to get a closer look.

"Can you help me?"

I froze in terror at the sound of a tiny voice. It was the voice of a little girl. *Oh my God . . .* I lifted my head and slowly turned my body to face the voice. I knew I was going to see her, though this horrified me. What would she look like? Would she be bloody? Like from a horror movie? I could feel her watching me, and the hair on my arms stood on end. Swallowing hard, I closed my eyes and then opened them.

There she was, plain as day. She was standing directly in front of the doorway, head cocked, staring up at me with large and pleading brown eyes. I couldn't move, and uncontrollably began to utter inaudible sounds. She was the Hannah I had seen in my dreams, right down to the blue dress and black Mary Janes.

"Oh . . . oh my God . . ."

"Please, don't be scared."

"I c-can't . . ." I blubbered.

Tears ran down my face, and I walked backward until I hit the wall and couldn't go any farther. Terrified, I covered my face with my hands, slid my back down the wall, and buried my face in my knees. Warm tears flowed down my cheeks. I just sat there, losing track of all time, and cried. Maybe I cried because I was scared, maybe because I felt sorry for Hannah, or maybe because I knew she was dead. All of those made sense. For some reason, huddling against the back wall as far away from the doorway as I could made me feel safe from harm. But yet, there wasn't anything to fear. Was there? I wasn't really scared of her; I was just scared of the fact that she was a ghost. And yet, who was being the coward here? It certainly wasn't *Hannah*. Who was I to shy away from her when she had just asked me for help? I gathered up the meager courage I had and tightened my chest. Slowly, moving my hands from my face, I opened my eyes. And there she was again. I didn't know what to say. What could I say? What did I *need* to say?

"Why are you scared of me?" Tears brimmed in her eyes. "What did I do?"

To my surprise, I began to talk, "You . . . you didn't scare me.

I mean, yes, you *did*, but not *intentionally*."

"What does that mean?"

"Oh, I'm sorry, I just . . . it means that you didn't do anything wrong. It's all me. Don't worry."

"Why are you crying?"

For a ghost, she's sure asking a lot of questions.

"I'm just really tired, and . . . I thought I was the only one here."

What kind of an answer was that? I'm just tired. Can ghosts read our minds? Does she know that I'm lying? Stupid!

Looking down at my knees, I asked her what I needed to know, "Is your name Hannah?"

"Yes."

"Hannah, h-have you been trying to reach me? Communicate with me?"

"Yes," she said again, this time lowering her head and wiping tears from her eyes. My heart wept for this little girl—she looked so sad and alone. Yet, at the same time, she looked strong for someone so young. Her face, however soft and sweet, showed signs of struggle and heartache—too much for such a young girl to have to bear.

"Why are you crying? And . . . why do you need my help?"

"I'm so scared . . ."

"What are you scared of, Hannah?"

"I'm scared of being alone. I don't want to be alone anymore. I want to be back with my family."

I didn't know what to say, but I knew I didn't want to lose her. There were too many questions that needed answers. "What do you want from me? How can I *help* you?"

She looked at me as if she was trying to reach my soul, and for a split second, I think she did. Then she began to walk toward me. I wanted to escape her path—the thought of her coming any closer scared the hell out of me. But I couldn't look away. Her innocence was captivating, and my limbs fell limp in her trusting gaze. Her large eyes were fathomless pits of the most beautiful brown, and her mouth curved at the corners to form the most adorable little pout. But her skin was deathly pale, despite the soft glow of pink in her cheeks. I was unable to move, my eyes helplessly fixated on her small figure. Once she reached me, she stopped, and then said in a small voice, "Take my hand."

I woke up the next morning in my own bed. It was still early, and I could sense that I was the only one awake. How, and when, did I get back here? Completely stupefied, I sat up. Then I thought about what had happened last night. Hannah . . . I saw Hannah last night, up in that room. But what happened? She'd walked toward me, and then . . . I took her hand and . . .

I closed my eyes tight, focusing hard. I remembered taking her hand in mine, and then there was darkness . . . until the images appeared. The images! How could I have *forgotten* them? Through our touch, she'd shared flashbacks of her life with me.

First, there was an image of a lady smiling down at her. Yes, her mom—that was Hannah's mom. Her mom and dad were standing next to her, smiling down. They looked so happy as they pointed to this house from the street. Then they were walking up the stairs, and led Hannah into the room on the right—Ben's room!

I gasped for a second and opened my eyes. *That was her room all along.* The clarity at which I was seeing the images now in my mind was incredible. It was as if it was happening for the first time all over again.

Then she was laughing and twirling around in a tutu, her little ballet shoes softly tapping along the kitchen floor. Her mom was making dinner, smiling at her from the kitchen counter. Her hair was furling around her, brushing her soft cheeks. And between the soft chunks of hair, I could see her twinkling eyes and her little red mouth—she was laughing, full of happiness.

Then I saw an image of the lady calling out to her from the deck. She had a smile on her face, but it wasn't a nice smile—it was contorted and sinister. She almost looked unreal—a dark force of some sort. A witch? I knew it; I felt it in my whole being. She wasn't a good witch, though. I knew good witches—Megan was a self-proclaimed witch. Something had happened to this witch—someone had taken something from her, but it wasn't Hannah. It *had* been in this house, though—in that room—and she wanted it back.

Hannah was running away from her. Then, there was darkness. I could hear her parents' voices as they called the police. A missing person report was filed. Where had Hannah gone?

Suddenly, I saw a book. An ancient book of spells of some sort? It had been opened. Someone had used it to steal what the witch wanted back . . . something dangerously enticing. And then I saw this person's face and my jaw dropped. Now it all seemed to make sense—the escalation of fame and good fortune. It had gotten way out of hand, though, and Hannah had paid the price for their recklessness. I knew what had to happen, but it seemed so far-fetched.

As I was coming to my wits, one last image surfaced—Hannah slowly turning around to meet my gaze. But when we were face to face, it was me I saw! I was so thin, the skin on my face was tight and pale, and my eyes looked like huge cloudy marbles. I reached out my hand as if asking for help . . .

Horrified, I shook my head to get the vision out of my mind. Then, glancing at the table beside my bed, I saw a black book. It was massive and ominous. It looked decades—no, centuries—old. The binding barely held it together and the pages were all crinkled and almost burnt at the edges. There was an intricate design on the cover—some creature with horns. *Is this the book of spells?* Whatever it was, it was . . .

"Hey, Jess. Catch!" In haste, I threw a dirty hoodie on top of the book to hide it from sight.

The baseball Ben threw at me whizzed past my face. "Tell me you didn't just *miss* that," he griped.

"Ben, I *just* woke up! What the hell are you *doing*?!" I shooed him away. "Get outta here!"

"*Sorry!*"

"Just . . . don't do that again!"

"*Fine.* I just wanted to play, that's all." He shuffled his feet, mumbling.

After a pause, I asked, "Ben, do you like it here?"

"Of course—don't *you*?"

"Yeah, I do. But sometimes it kinda creeps me out."

He shot me a weird glance. "*What* creeps you out?"

"I don't know, like, the history of this place, I guess. That's really the only thing that gets to me." Sighing, I stared ahead, feeling lost and helpless.

"You wanna go outside?"

"Outside . . . *now*? But it's so early."

"I know, but I'm bored."

Begrudgingly, "Okay, fine. Let's go."

The sun was beginning its slow ascent, and our backyard glimmered with luxurious oranges and golds. It made me think about our backyard on Crescent Lane, and the way it looked the morning we'd left. We sat down on the chairs. I had my arms crossed, and Ben was slouched over with his elbows on his knees.

"What was their name—the family who lived here before us? Do you know?" he asked.

"The Crawfords."

"Do you think they were nice people?"

"I do."

"How do you know?"

"Mmm, call it a feeling. But I also feel, like . . . well, something bad happened here, and it needs to be fixed."

His face turned pale. "W-what do you mean?"

"I mean just that. Just be careful, okay?"

"Okay . . ." his voice faltered.

There was silence as we both sat there ruminating. I could feel the tension, and I didn't like it. I'd already said too much. These were my demons to deal with, not his. And I had to keep him as far away from this as possible.

11

Megan Leads the Way

That Sunday night, I called Amy and Max from the phone in my room.

"Oh my God, you actually *saw* her?" Amy asked, horrified.

"Yes, clear as day. And I talked to her. It was so . . . surreal."

"Wow," I heard Max on the other end. "I can't believe you actually saw her. What did she *say* to you?"

"She was asking me for help, and then she told me she was scared of being alone."

"Help? What does she want you to do? Did she *say*?" Amy asked.

"No, she didn't say anything. She just . . . she reached out her hand to me and I grabbed it."

"Reached out her hand? What the hell? She's a ghost—how are you even supposed to touch it? Don't you, like, just go through her? Aren't ghosts just vapor?" Amy was stupefied.

"No, that's the weirdest thing. I grabbed her hand and . . . I could feel it."

"What happened?" Max asked.

"It was like scenes from her life flashed before me, but I just saw tiny fragments. She was happy, laughing, dancing . . . and then all the sudden, there's a witch and this ancient book of some sort. And something was stolen from the witch's realm. I know this all sounds insane, but you guys *have* to believe me!"

"A witch? Something stolen?" I could just feel Max's fear and excitement. "Guys, this is *nuts*. This is . . . how do you know all this, Jess?"

"It was all flashbacks—when I took her hand, my mind was flooded with them. Then, after the flashbacks . . . I saw something *really* scary."

"What'd you see?"

"I saw Hannah, in front of me . . . And when she turned around, it was me! And I was so thin . . . my skin was so pale, and my *eyes* were the worst part—they were almost popping out of my head like huge marbles. And I reached out my hand as if I needed help . . . it was horrible! God, it was *so scary!*" I started to cry.

"Oh, Jess . . . that's *horrifying!*" Amy cried.

"I know! And what does it *mean?* Am I safe? Because that *really* scares me, and I keep thinking something awful is going to happen to me now." I began sobbing harder.

"No, no . . . Jess, please. You're fine. It's just a vision. It was probably brought on by everything else going on right now. I mean, with all the crazy stuff that's been happening . . . It's fine, and you have us. So don't worry . . . you're safe."

"Thanks, Max." I wiped the tears from my face.

"Hey, we got your back, Jess," Amy said.

"Thanks . . . I don't know what I'd do without you guys."

"Friends forever," Max said.

"Friends forever," I whimpered back.

"I know what we have to do though. I know who stole from

the witch's realm. And the more I think about it . . . if we don't do this, I could be next. I'll need your help, and Megan's."

The next week was a trying one for me. I was rattled from the weekend as it was, and then on Thursday Matt Kingston opened up a can of worms.

"Hey, Jess, I heard you got a ghost in your attic," he whispered to me.

"Where'd you hear that? I don't have a *ghost* in my attic."

"Oh yeah? That's not what I heard your friends saying earlier."

"Matt, *c'mon*! God . . . Okay, *yes*! You happy? And now, thanks to you, probably the whole school knows."

"Well, only like . . ." He shrugged. "Yeah, you're probably right."

"Thanks. *So* nice of you. *Really.*"

"Hey."

"What?"

"Maybe the little girl's parents hid her up in the attic, and they cut her up . . . alive! Then they stuffed her remains in the wall."

I coiled in disgust. *"What?!"*

"Haven't you heard her screams at night? Rumor is she wants revenge, and she won't leave that house until she gets it."

"Stop it, *stop it*!" I slammed my desk. Miss Peterson shot up from her chair, stunned.

"Jess! What on earth is going on?"

Then with cool, steely eyes, she gazed at Matt, who was sitting there twiddling his thumbs and casually looking around.

"Matt, do you have anything to do with this?"

"What? I was just telling Jess a funny story." Then he leaned over and cupped his hand to the side of his mouth, practically yelling as he spoke, "There's a ghost, evil as they come, livin' in that ole house of hers. Just tellin' her to stay safe, that's all.

Lookin' out for her, you know." He winked.

"Matt, to the principal's office!" He stared at her, mouth agape. "*Now!*" She pointed sharply to the door.

"Geez, I was just *kiddin'*." Then turning to me, "Sorry, Jess. Didn't mean to scare ya. Wuss."

"You're such a dumbass."

"*Jess!*"

"Sorry, Miss Peterson."

Matt got up and swaggered off, always needing to be the center of attention.

I could feel my face turning red—it had to be red as an apple right now. Tears threatened to blur my vision. Miss Peterson shot me a sweet smile, and I reciprocated. But underneath my smile, I was terrified. And also, a little . . . excited. *It's not going to be me next, shit for brains.*

Thank goodness the morning flew by. "Why don't you talk to what's-her-face again?" Amy asked at lunch.

"Who's *what's-her-face?*"

"You know, that girl in your art class. Goth chic."

"Oh, yeah, Megan. I didn't get a chance to talk to her in art class today, so I'll see if I can catch her at her locker later."

"Yeah, isn't she the one who told you to go up there in the first place?"

"She was, and I think I have a plan in place. I mean, it's pretty rough right now, but I know what has to be done. It's just gonna be hard to do."

"Well, you told us who did it—doesn't he have a crush on her? I mean, his girlfriend's nice and everything, but she's kinda cookie-cutter. *Boring.* Megan, though—um, *boring* is the last word I'd use to describe her." Max was onto something, and it turned out Megan could help me more than I'd thought. Hell, she could run circles around him. She had more smarts in her pinky than he did in his entire brain.

Just then, the bell rang. "Let us know how it goes with Megan."

"I will, Amy. See ya guys." I threw away my lunch leftovers and headed to Megan's locker.

"What?" Megan stared at me wide-eyed, mouth agape after I told her what happened. "You made a connection—you touched the other side. Do you know how *incredible* that is?"

While I couldn't help but be concerned about what happened to that poor little girl, all Megan could think about was the act itself. Couldn't blame her; this was her territory, after all.

"I know, I know . . . but listen."

"Okay . . . But seriously—you know how *amazing* this is, right?!"

I'd never seen Megan this excited before about *anything*. Just then, I had an outlandish thought about her producing a crazy paranormal show on television where people record their encounters with ghosts in old buildings and haunted houses.

"Yes, I do, but that's not what I'm really thinking about. Megan, something bad happened to that little girl—something *really* bad—and it happened in that house. *Our* house!"

As I said this, the hair on my arms stood on end and a shiver ran down my spine. Involuntarily, I shook it off.

"Well, you need to find out what that is."

"But that's just it—I need your help because I *know* what happened." I told her all about my visions and the stolen book.

"Oh, wow . . . So what do you want me to do?"

"Well, we need to get him *there*. To *my* house, in that room, with that book."

"Pfft, consider it done."

"What? Just like that?"

"Just like that. I have my ways."

"Yeah, I figured. Oh . . . but don't think. I mean, I didn't mean it *that* way."

"It's okay, I know . . . Jess, you're gonna be *so* happy! My aunt used to conduct séances, so I know this stuff. Oh man, this is gonna be so much fun!" She looked as if she'd practically gone mad in her guileless excitement. Her eyes were darting this way and that like her mind was in overdrive, grabbing bits and pieces of information here and there, sorting and planning.

A séance? Really? Good Lord, Jess, what are you getting yourself into?

"Do we really need a *séance*? I mean, does there really have to be any kind of ritual?"

"Well, no, but . . . I don't know. Maybe? This will be my first encounter with the paranormal. My first *real* encounter," she placed her hands on her chest as if she was accepting some kind of award.

"I wish I were as excited about this as you are, believe me."

"Then *be* excited. What's stopping you?"

"An overwhelming sense of dread, that's what. You don't know, Megan. You don't know the feelings I've been feeling. Like, I don't know what's going to happen. *Anything* could happen! Why are we even *doing* this?? Shouldn't I hire a professional?"

"You'll be fine, Jess." She gently placed her hand on my shoulder. "You'll see—everything will be fine. We'll solve this together, and get things back to normal."

"I hope you're right, Megan. I hope you're right . . ."

The next day at lunch, I told Max and Amy about Megan coming over and our plan. We chose Friday night because my parents would be home after midnight and Ben was sleeping over at a friend's house. I didn't know how Megan was going to get *him* to my place, but I trusted her.

"Told you she knew her stuff," Max said. "That girl is like the kid from *The Shining*."

"Ha, ain't that the truth." Amy laughed.

"Well, that's not a *bad* thing in this situation."

Max nodded to Amy. "We didn't say it was, Jess—did we, Ames?"

"No, Megan's just *different*, that's all."

"I know, she's like, a total one-eighty from you two. But she really knows a lot about this stuff, and I think we're actually gonna get somewhere this time. I mean, I'm scared as hell to go back up there again, but it's gotta be done. The only thing is, Megan said you guys shouldn't come up with us."

"What? What kinda *BS* is that?" Max scoffed.

"Max, c'mon, you *know* you and Amy are my best friends—and believe me, I wish you could come too. But Megan said the fewer people, the better. And having you guys there might prevent Hannah from even showing up at all."

"Well, at least Megan's gonna be there," Amy said. "What if Hannah doesn't show up with Megan there, though? What'll you do then?"

"She'll show up—the energy will be right. I just know it. I think last time, I blocked out some things Hannah was trying to communicate to me. She might be able to pick up on some things I don't. Besides, he'll be there too and he's the missing link."

"This is pretty deep, isn't it?" Max was leaning toward me, chin on her palm.

"Yeah, I guess so."

The bell rang, catching us by surprise.

"Well, see you guys later. And thanks for understanding."

"But of course. What are friends for?" Max quipped.

After dinner that day, I helped clean up and then went to my bedroom. I just wanted to be alone with my thoughts for a little while. This was really happening again, and everything was laid out. And the fact that Megan was doing this for me this time was really, really cool. She didn't have to. Although, of course, I understood why she wanted to do this personally. Who knows, maybe she'd become a good friend too? Or maybe I was just jumping ahead of myself. Either way, she was helping me out and that felt good. I couldn't have asked for more.

The next day at school, I couldn't concentrate. It was Friday, and all I could think about was what Megan and I were planning to do tonight. If I was to find out how to help Hannah and how to fix this, then Megan was my winning ticket. In art class, she told me about what she was planning. She was a novice in séances, for sure, but felt confident she'd get the answers we needed.

"Hannah might show up, but she might not, so we'll be using a Ouija board."

"A *Ouija* board?!"

"Yes, this is important—I'm going to be Hannah's medium, and she'll use me to answer our questions."

"Okay, but you're freakin' me out. Maybe I've just watched too many scary movies . . . I don't know. I mean, do we *really* need a Ouija board? What if we summon that witch by accident? What if we're all transported to that realm and get stuck there?"

"Pfft . . . Hollywood sensationalizes this stuff, Jess. Don't think about that. This is not a movie, this is real life . . . *your* life."

"I know, but I almost feel like I'm outside looking in. Sometimes it's just really . . . unbelievable."

"I hear ya, but it's a pretty *awesome* unbelievable." She playfully nudged me. "I mean, we're gonna be communicating with a spirit tonight who has a story to tell. She needs someone to listen and she's chosen you. You're the chosen one."

I laughed. "It's like I have some superpower or something."

Megan didn't laugh. "Yeah, pretty much. Hannah could have left you alone if she wanted to. Yes, she talked to Ben, but only because she wanted to get to *you*. And maybe because that was her old room too—who knows? But she wants you to help her because she trusts you and she believes in you. Now that's some pretty powerful stuff, if you ask me."

"I guess so." I scratched my head. "But what if what she's asking for is too much? What if it's something I'm not able to do?"

Megan stared at me sternly. "That's a bridge we'll cross when we need to. Baby steps."

"I guess you're right. No sense in getting worked up about this too soon." I laughed. "Easier said than done though." *Baby steps, Jess. Baby steps . . .*

"Are you going to be okay?" Amy asked at the end of English class.

"I'll be fine," I assured her. "You guys don't have to worry about me."

They looked at me, concerned.

"Jess, Megan seems cool and all, but we don't really *know* her. I mean, do *you* really know her?"

"What's there to know? It's not like she's some psycho or something. She likes to dabble in the occult and she's fascinated by the spirit world. I don't see anything wrong with that. I . . .

I think it's kinda cool."

They shot me strange stares.

"Hey, am I hearing this right? Has Megan Pierce become a close friend of Jess Kierney? Because, last I checked . . ." Max said as she pointed to herself and Amy, "*we* were your closest friends."

"You guys, oh my God—are you *jealous*? C'mon! There's nothing to be jealous about. Megan could never replace you two!"

"Okay, just checkin'," Max said, arms crossed and looking to the side.

"You guys are ridiculous."

"*Max* is the ridiculous one. I'm fine," Amy quipped.

"What the?!" Max pushed Amy in her chair. "What a liar, Amy! Back me up here, will ya?"

"Okay, you're just a just *teensy* bit." She held her hand up with her forefinger almost touching her thumb.

"Thank you," Max bowed her head, even though that wasn't much of a compliment.

"*Very funny*. But seriously—enough, you guys! We're going to do this tonight whether you like it or not. But I appreciate your support and I know you have my back, so thank you."

12

The Séance

I hugged my parents goodbye for the night before they left for dinner and a concert with friends. There was silence as the door closed, and a strange emptiness filled me—it felt as if I couldn't move. I was standing there, submerged in my own thoughts, when the phone rang in the kitchen.

"We're on our way," Amy said.

I took a deep breath, closed my eyes, and opened them as fierce determination set in.

A few minutes later, Amy and Max showed up at the door. I let them in and we just stood there looking at each other for what felt like an eternity.

"So, when are they getting here?" Amy asked.

"They should be here any minute." Just then, the doorbell rang. "It's showtime . . ."

"*Beetlejuice!*" Max nervously blurted out. She loved that line in the movie—who didn't?

I opened the door to welcome Megan and Matt in. Matt had the faint smell of alcohol on him. And as I was about to close the door, Josh Potter stepped in. Wide-eyed, I stepped back and almost tripped over myself. Josh chuckled and Matt covered his mouth and pointed at me, smirking.

"Not happy to see me?" Josh quipped.

Just then, Megan shot me a wink. *That little* . . . how had she arranged this? Her powers were beyond my comprehension.

"Let's get this started, shall we?" Matt put his arms around Megan and me and winked. Gross . . .

Megan's hair had always been dyed black, except for a few strands in the front that were now dyed purple, running in perfect stripes along the sides of her face. She was wearing darker eyeliner than usual, which turned up slightly at the corners of her eyes, and was dressed from head to toe in black.

"Well hold on a sec, Matt," Megan cooed. "Let's not rush. Whatcha got in that backpack of yours?"

"Oh, well, you said it was gonna be a séance, so I brought one of my *favorite books*." He reached into his backpack and pulled out a book that looked as ancient as the one I had in my bedroom, but this one was even *more* disturbing. It looked like death itself and had a stench to it, almost like garbage.

"What the . . ." Josh said under his breath.

"Yeah, this is my secret weapon. This little baby has brought me a ton of luck. I don't know what I'd do without her."

Max and Amy shot me a *what the hell* look, and Megan stared me dead in the eye.

"W-where did you get that, Matt?" I stuttered.

"Where do you *think* I got it? From the *library*?"

Max sighed and rolled her eyes.

"Forgive my friend here—he forgot his manners." Josh jabbed Matt in the side with his elbow.

"*Sorry*," Matt mumbled, looking away.

I led them to the kitchen, and we all sat at the table.

Amy broke the awkward silence. "So how'd you get so into this stuff, Megan? You know, the paranormal?"

"Well, for me, it's just an escape from the real world. I mean, so many people live in their superficial worlds with their superficial friends and they . . . they create *drama*. It's ridiculous and absurd. It's everywhere at school, and can drive you mad if you don't have an escape mechanism. So mine's the *beyond*, if you will. To me, it's peaceful. Reading about life after death and ghosts and spirits takes me to another world for a little bit—a world of possibilities and questions. Nobody really knows the answers, and that's the beauty of it. You can interpret it any way you want, and who's to say you're wrong?" She paused. "I just like that. I like the beautiful complexity."

She seemed regal in her certainty, and I envied her confidence.

"Well? What're we all doing here? Let's go see that *ghost!*" Matt laughed.

Megan sighed and rolled her eyes. "I guess it *is* time."

Megan and I told Max, Amy, and Josh to stay downstairs. After a few awkward glances at each other, they accepted their penance and sat down in the living room. The air was thick with uncertainty, fear, and tension. After scanning the comfort of the downstairs one last time, we headed upstairs to my room. I grabbed the ancient book off my nightstand along with my trusty flashlight. We went out to the hallway and stared at the door to the attic stairs for a minute. Fully aware of what kind of danger we could be getting ourselves into, we couldn't turn back. Not now.

With Megan and Matt standing on either side of me, I slowly turned the doorknob and opened the door. The cold draft of air washed over us and we stood there in awe staring up into darkness—three people who couldn't be more different from each other. It was almost humorous.

"*Shhh* . . . quiet!" I whispered loudly to Matt as we began ascending the staircase. He kept on hitting the steps with his sneakers.

"Sorry! Why the hell isn't there a light up here?" he grumbled. "This is so stupid."

"There's the landing. We're almost there." Suddenly, I froze.

"C'mon, Jess. What's wrong?" Megan asked.

"I'm just scared. I don't want to see her again. I don't . . ."

"Jess, it's fine."

She touched my shoulder. It felt comforting, and I was reminded again of what a good friend Megan had become. After all, she was doing this all for me. Sure, she had her motives too—she reveled in the supernatural and had fun getting scared, I guessed. But in the end, this was for me.

Shortly after, Megan snapped, "Matt, *stop* it!"

"Sorry, Megan. Your ass is right in front of me—what am I supposed to do?"

Jesus . . . I rolled my eyes. He was hopeless.

Then, visions of my last encounter with Hannah came to me. Turning around and seeing her there, reaching out to me and pleading for help. It was almost too much to bear—dreadful and unimaginable, but also inescapable and inevitable. I was drawn to her, no matter how scared I was. And there was no turning back. What was done was done. Sealed deal.

"Jess, you okay?" Megan asked.

"Yeah, I'm okay. We're almost there. Just a couple more steps."

And then, there we were, facing the door. It looked sinister as all hell and seemed to move and breathe as if it had a life of its own. It was beckoning us to come in.

"You ready, Jess? I'm not doing anything until you're ready."

"God, you're good at this."

"Good at what?"

"It's a compliment. You're just good at . . . at being here for me. I need you. I need your help. So, thank you. And thanks for coming too, Matt." Those last words slithered out of my mouth; but without him, this whole thing was a bust.

"Hey, I'm just along for the ride. Don't want to miss a séance in my old stomping grounds."

Turning in the dimly lit hallway, I asked, "Old stomping grounds, huh?"

"This book—I got it from this room. Before the Crawfords moved in, dark shit went on in this room. I heard stories, and I was feeling a little adventurous. So . . ." He held the book up, wiggling it and sporting a wide grin. "Breaking and entering, and no one knew a thing."

Just then, the doorknob turned and the door opened, hinges creaking eerily along.

"What the . . ."

"It did this before, Megan. I *hate* it when it does this."

I could feel some tension in Megan now. *About time . . .* Reaching my hand out, I slowly pushed the door all the way open. Soft moonlight filtered through again, but the room had a different energy tonight. It was unsettling. And though my gut told me to turn and run like hell back down those steps, I stood my ground. *Curiosity killed the cat.* Stepping inside ever so slowly, I noticed the room was completely different now. There was no small bed with a plush ruby comforter and no white desk. There was only a large circle of dark candles on the floor in the center of the room, softly throwing freakish shadows on the walls as they flickered.

We all cautiously stepped in, mesmerized by the haunting

scene before us. Just then, my flashlight went dark. It seemed the batteries were also too scared to function. I was gripped in fear. "Megan? This doesn't look good—"

Suddenly, the door slammed shut, and an unnerving hum began to reverberate inside the room. Then, a low growl emanated, seeming to rise from the depths and shaking the very walls that confined us.

"I want what's mine."

Megan dropped the Ouija board, and it was dragged ahead of us as if by an invisible hand, slowly lifted, and then shattered to pieces. Screaming, we ran for the door, trying desperately to open it, but to no avail. My heart was pounding in my chest. *Am I having a panic attack?* Megan tightly grabbed my hand and nodded her head to the center of the room. Matt had walked into the middle of the lit circle, holding the book he had brought out in front of him. Suddenly, the book I was holding began to writhe. With a scream, I dropped it, and it was dragged to the middle of the circle. It stopped in front of Matt.

"What say you, boy?"

"I . . . I . . ." We saw liquid pool around Matt's shoes. Just then, his head whipped back, his arms were thrown wide, and he was levitated into the air.

"How dare you steal from me."

I couldn't breathe. I didn't even know the last time I had. My entire body was as tense as a rubber band being pulled and stretched to its limits. How had this pure evil lurked in here all this time? How was this even happening? *And where was Hannah?*

To our horror, the candles began to flicker on and off. At first slowly, and then rapidly. As they did, the book Matt was holding slowly left his hand and started floating in front of him, glowing a deep red. Matt remained elevated in the air, paralyzed. He was making moaning sounds and seemed to be struggling to breathe. Then, what looked like some sort of portal appeared before us in a murky circle, the center of which we could see clearly. There was a ghastly bookcase on the other side with no end and no beginning. And there was something surrounding all the books—it was black and oozing. Several books glowed the same way Matt's did, but in different colors.

There was an empty space with a red glow that Matt's book slowly slid into. Then we heard a cackle that ran up the length of my spine. It was wicked, sharp, and full of vengeance. And suddenly, there was nothing to see but darkness as the candles extinguished.

I screamed a guttural scream that shook my entire body—loud, hard, and anguished. I heard Megan's fingers scrawling over the door behind us, trying to find the doorknob. Then confusion as the doorknob began wriggling. We backed away and the door was flung open. I instinctively fled out of the darkness and into . . . an embrace. Looking up, I saw Josh Potter's face in the soft glow of the flashlight Max was holding. It was full of fear and confusion. I wept into his flannel shirt as he hugged me tightly.

13

Epilogue

The next day, Hannah's parents heard the doorbell ring. Her mom answered the door, and immediately let out an exalted cry and began to sob uncontrollably. Her husband heard this and ran to the door to see her kneeling and hugging their daughter Hannah, who had been gone for over a year. She was wearing the same beautiful blue dress she had worn for her dance recital the day she'd disappeared. Some way, somehow, their baby had come home. Bewildered and elated, he rushed to hug his little girl.

The search for Matt's body had been going on for the past month to no avail. The town of Westmont was ripped apart by yet another tragedy. But there was also celebration for a beautiful and unexplainable miracle. Police were still investigating and questioning, trying to arrive at a theory. Yet they'd come no closer to the truth. All Hannah could tell them was that it was dark and scary, and she was alone. Her memory was foggy, and she couldn't remember anything specific. And apparently, Matt had told no one he had come to my house that night.

We thought about telling the police what happened but doubted they would believe us. There was a vengeful witch of some sort who had swapped Hannah's soul for Matt's? In my own house? No . . . it was futile. We hoped that somewhere, somehow, Matt was still with us; but it was impossible to know.

I spent my days as I always had, with my besties Amy and Max. But our close-knit group had expanded with the addition of Megan and my boyfriend, Josh. We still didn't talk about that night much, and when we did, we felt gnawing guilt mixed with divine retribution. Matt's disappearance weighed heavily on us, but Hannah's return was sublime. Had we known what was going to happen, of course, we would have planned that night differently . . . but how? The book of spells that had appeared by my bed was the only thing left in the room after Matt disappeared. Even the remnants of the Ouija board had vanished. In a rage, Josh had picked the book up, ran into the backyard, and thrown it into the forest.

I did know one thing, though—the evil that had been lurking in our house was gone now. My dad had moved some odds and ends into that room up by the attic, and I'd even found the courage to visit again myself. Nothing happened, and I felt no negative energy. It was the first time in my life that "nothing" felt good.

As the onset of summer blessed us with warm, sunny days and those absolutely perfect nights, my friends and I enjoyed our time on the deck catching up on the latest and greatest. And as we were discussing our plans for the summer one Saturday evening, just as the sun was beginning to set, Megan sat up tall and cocked her head toward the forest. "Did you guys hear that?"

"Hear what?" Max asked, perplexed.

"I swear, someone just said your name, Jess . . . you guys didn't hear that?"

"Um, *no*. You okay, Megan?"

"Jess, I'm serious! Stop joking a—"

"Jess . . ." It was ever so faint, but I heard it this time and it made my skin crawl. The voice seemed to reverberate in the air. Slowly, I looked behind me, trembling with fear. Amy and Max froze. "What the . . ."

"What do we do, guys? We should go inside," Amy's face was pale and her wide eyes filled with fear.

"No. We go find this jackass who thinks they're so *goddamn funny*." Megan stood up and, in unspoken agreement, we all joined her.

Slowly, in unison with Megan at the helm, we walked down the steps of the deck onto the grass which seemed to be a minefield now—every step bringing us closer to danger. Huddled together, we were prepared to strike or flee at any moment. As we followed the voice, we found ourselves getting closer to the small pine trees where I had first found the porcelain doll. With every step, the voice grew clearer and more distinct. It was the voice of a boy.

And as we reached the pine trees, I stopped in my tracks, gasped, and covered my mouth with my hands. There, laying in the same spot as before, was another porcelain doll. How long it had been here was impossible to know.

"Jess, that's . . . Isn't this where you found *Hannah's* doll?" Max's voice was muted and distant, drowned out by the fear rising inside me. The doll was wearing the same clothes Matt Kingston had worn the night we'd planned the séance. I knew because he was wearing that same red hoodie, torn jeans, and striped sneakers.

We all stood there staring midst the silence of dusk—shocked, scared, and confused. All that could be heard was the sweet melody of crickets, which sounded like drumbeats now. And we stared as if in a trance until the voice came again, emanating from the doll before us.

"Jess . . . help . . . me . . ."

Overcome with bewilderment, we also full well knew whose voice it was.

"What's . . .? Do you guys see that? That light?" Max pointed toward the forest.

From within the writhing brush before us, a bright light glowed, beautiful in its soft tone. It was lavender in color, and I could tell it was near the edge, not too far in.

"What the hell *is* that?" Amy squinted, confused.

"Is that? It can't be . . ."

"Can't be what, Jess?" Amy asked, perplexed.

"The book of spells . . . Josh threw it in here that night. I saw him do it. It was *right here* . . . What else *could* it be?" Megan surmised, with arms crossed.

I let out a slow exhale and closed my eyes. "It's not over."

"No, it's not. And he needs us," Megan whispered.

Max exhaled and shook her head, "Well, shit, here we go again . . ."

"You guys ready to save another soul?" Megan asked. "I mean, his soul always needed saving anyway."

"That's not funny," Amy scoffed.

"But it's true," I replied.

Amy looked to Max for support, but Max just shrugged. We could all hear Amy's exasperated sigh as she then held Max's hand. Max looked at me and held my hand, and I then held

Megan's.

And there it was . . . the energy inside all of us shifted. I could feel its transformation fill the air around us. It was electrifying. No one had said anything, but a mutual understanding could be felt—one of bold determination. We stood tall facing the ominous light that was beckoning us to enter.

Just four girls, on a mission to save another soul.

About the Author

Janelle Schiecke lives with her husband, her son, and their two cats. This is her first published book, and she has always reveled in ghost stories and everything spooky. Though she began her career editing trade magazines and historical nonfiction, she presently enjoys writing scary books with enjoyable characters which readers can connect with.

When she is not writing, Janelle enjoys spending time with her family and friends, catching up on the latest streaming series and movies, and planning her next family travel adventure.

www.ingramcontent.com/pod-product-compliance
Lightning Source LLC
Chambersburg PA
CBHW022032170626
46808CB00003B/1163